All Through the Night

A WELSH WESTERN

Neil Thomas

D1396316

THORO*g*OOD

Published by Thorogood
10-12 Rivington Street
London EC2A 3DU

Telephone: 020 7749 4748
Fax: 020 7729 6110
Email: info@thorogoodpublishing.co.uk
Web: www.thorogoodpublishing.co.uk

A CIP catalogue record for this book is available from
the British Library.

ISBN paperback: 978 185418 8960
ISBN eBook: 978 185418 8977

Printed and bound in Great Britain by
Marston Book Services Ltd

To my Welsh ancestors:
the stories they told and the songs they sang

Also to Cheryl, Ella and Amy for indulging me when
I bathe my Welsh roots in the warm waters of nostalgia

And in memory of my father

For far too long, the Americans have had the monopoly on the Wild West of cowboys, trailhands, rawhide and cattle drives.

However, as this tale shows, this Wild West did not 'come out of nowhere', as it were.

The familiar story of cattle drives – in the sense beloved of Westerns – really originates in the UK, with the drovers who brought cattle, sheep, goats, turkeys, geese and pigs to the towns from far-flung rural areas of Scotland, the West Country and Wales.

Maybe crossing the Menai Strait doesn't have quite the same cachet as crossing the Rio Grande, but everything we've come to expect of a good Western happened in Britain, only many years before.

From the Wild West of Wales, it is also tempting to think that we exported the very notion of cowboys – Americans are much more literal – but we called them drovers.

The fictional events in this novel take place in the late eighteenth century, perhaps the heyday for cattle drives from Wales to London as well as for the popularity of Welsh music and poetry in the capital. For example, a book entitled *Musical and Poetical Relicks of the Welsh Bards* was published in London in 1794 as a three-volume work by Edward Jones (1752 – 1824), a Welsh harpist, bard, performer, composer, arranger and collector of music.

The language throughout is English, ignoring the fact that a lot of it would have been in Welsh, especially, of course, the old songs.

———— ◆ ————

The English lyrics for the Welsh songs used in this book are based on those appearing alongside the older, Welsh lyrics in *The Songs of Wales (Royal Edition)*, published in the nineteenth century and edited by Brinley Richards.

The monologue in Chapter 10 was written down by my father having been passed down through previous generations by oral tradition.

PART ONE

1

RIDING HIS WELSH COB OUT of the water and across the sand, Rhys has his back to a narrow strip of shallow sea. He looks up in wonder at the panorama ahead of him. As if accompanied by sweeping music, he sees Snowdon in the distance surrounded by its mountain ranges, slowly being shrouded in melancholic clouds of rain and mist as the weather closes in.

He wheels round quickly so that he now faces the fast-flowing waters of the Menai Strait and looks over to the far bank, to Anglesey.

There, about a quarter of a mile away, he sees his father – a white-haired old man of dignified bearing – standing next to the young black-haired and fiery-eyed woman Rhys is betrothed to. Alongside them is a small bunch of black-clothed men that looks like a small herd rather than a choral group at this distance.

He hears, floating across the water, the voices of the dozen-or-so-strong male voice choir that seem to take up the tune he has been hearing in his head as they sing *All Through the Night*.

> *Love, fear not if sad thy dreaming*
> *All through the night,*
> *Though o'ercast, bright stars are gleaming*
> *All through the night.*
> *Joy will come to thee at morning,*
> *Life with sunny hope adorning,*
> *Though sad dreams may give dark warning*
> *All through the night.*
>
> *Angels watching ever round thee*
> *All through the night,*
> *In thy slumbers close surround thee*
> *All through the night.*
> *They should of all fear disarm thee,*
> *No forebodings should alarm thee,*
> *They will let no peril harm thee,*
> *All through the night.*

Rhys then sees a dark mass visible in the water and he slowly picks out the herd of Welsh Black cattle, led by the oldest of the cows, swimming towards him for the near shore. He sees one animal, much smaller, losing its way at the back and returning to the far, home shore and wonders what that might symbolise for the start of their long drove to London.

He looks closely at the herd and the cattle are variously thrashing about, with men in rowing boats shouting in Welsh and English trying to direct operations without too much success. There are dogs – corgis and border collies, some in the boats barking and some in the water swimming furiously.

It is a scene of total chaos and, almost in spite of the efforts of the men and the dogs in the boats and in the water, their shouts of encouragement and anger and their attempts at throwing ropes round the horns of some of the cattle to try and tow them across, somehow progress across the wild stretch of water does seem to be being made.

The only calm spot is the boat at the rear, methodically being rowed across, which contains some of their provisions for the journey as well as ferrying over, in relative comfort, the travellers who would be tagging along with them on the journey for company and safety.

Rhys, knowing that because of the shifting tides there is only a half-hour slot, at most, for the crossing to be completed successfully, glances anxiously across again to the distant shore and sees the 'lost' runt standing near the choir, his girl and his father — all forming a fitting farewell tableau.

2

Three weeks earlier

IN THEIR COSY FARMHOUSE KITCHEN, Rhys, as black-haired as his father is white-haired, but otherwise with the same square jaw and Roman nose, sits on the other side of the hearth from his father, Caradog. The lamb and leek soup in a pot on the range is bubbling merrily away as Caradog puffs on his clay pipe, their two black and white border collies asleep at his feet in front of the fire.

Caradog takes his pipe out of his mouth.

'It'll be Honesty Jones's last drive to London. I still think of him as a young man, mind, for I've got ten years at least on him, but he feels he's now getting, like me, too old for the arduous work alone and he misses the days when he and I would set out together, with Smithfield as the journey's end.'

'He was, it's true, very frightened the last drove he did, what with him carrying so much money, when they were lucky to miss that highwayman who robbed and killed another drover, and only the day before Honesty passed the self-same way.'

'This is why you've now to take up the droving duties, or we risk losing our livelihood.'

'I can see that, but I'm happy on the farm raising the animals. Anyway, I've Eunice to think about and our future.'

'Eunice knows and understands.'

'You've spoken to her about this, behind my back?'

'I know what she means to you and I wanted to square it with her first. Only with her support will this work.'

'She wants me here. I want to be here. I've the Bard's crown at the eisteddfod to work towards. Why can't we do what other farmers do and let other men do our droving? And, as he's keen to do it, we could let Guto take over.'

'You lose control doing that. The money is cut too many ways. Better to drive our own animals and do that, for a price, of course, for our loyal friends as well. Our family has made its name and its money doing it this way. Will you try it this time with Drover Jones? You might enjoy learning the ropes from him and seeing London.'

'I've done the journey before you know, once, when I was a boy, and I didn't enjoy it one bit.'

'You're older now and wiser, I hope. And you'd be partnering a master and learning from him. If we take him up on his offer, he'll carry on for a while until he thinks you're ready to take over. He's a true and faithful friend to us. Not for nothing is Drover Jones's nickname Honesty. By the way, he also says he doesn't think he can really trust Guto to do it, so he wants us to take over from him and to handle his lucrative trade of carrying money and legal documents for the farmers around here and doing all kinds of business transactions on their behalf.'

'I'd be hopeless at that. The only notes I care about are musical, not promissory ones.'

'There'll be time enough for poetry and music when you've made a success of this. Look, I don't want to play this card, but I've thought about this long and hard and frankly, I'll not be here much longer.'

'That's blackmail – totally unfair. You're right on one thing: you shouldn't be playing that card, not with me.'

'I want to know that you can do it and carry on here. You speak English fluently, which is a huge advantage when it comes to haggling and in winning the trust of the people you'll hope to deal with. In a few years, when you're thirty and married, you can get your droving licence and you'll be set up for the future. Droving has taught me so much about people and life – seeing the towns and London itself with its culture and its crowds just makes you glad you have been there, even if you're gladder still to have come back.'

Later that evening

Caradog, now alone and no longer having to keep up appearances, crumples and settles back in his chair by the fireside. Half asleep, he remembers back to the early days, when he and a very young Honesty were starting out as drovers working the route to London.

Suddenly, in his reverie, he clearly sees the gnarled face of Pagan Evans, the head drover who had taught them everything really.

Before he knows it, he hears himself saying out loud to the empty room:

'And to think I could've taken your advice, Pagan.'

He thinks of the ferocious rows he and Honesty used to have with Pagan, and between themselves towards the end, before they eventually took over the droving routes and Pagan moved on.

He had grown tired of the harsh travelling and all the uncertainty of the trade and had urged Caradog and Honesty to join him in slate quarrying, of all things, and leave the droving trade.

'How different life might have been,' Caradog again voices out loud. 'None of the long absences... leaving behind others we cared about, to cope as best they could without us... me not being there when she needed me most... and then, of course, there'd be no pressure on Rhys to take over when his heart isn't really in it...'

He shakes his head to try and stop his mind going to painful places and reminds himself that although Pagan had wound up as a foreman for Lord Penrhyn in the slate works – a regular job, yes – in the end, it was a miserable one.

Pagan had always had his wits about him, that was for sure, and it was a shock that in the year before he died, he'd told Honesty there wasn't a day that went by that he didn't miss being on the road and in charge of his own destiny.

He'd built up a fortune for the Penrhyn family, but in the end he didn't even own his own home. Some said Pagan's slate quarry was the largest in the world – a tribute to his skills for sure, even if he himself had precious little to show for the achievement.

'To the victor, the spoils,' sighs Caradog, 'to the toilers the spoil,' he continues aloud. 'Poor old Pagan. He deserved better than that. At least Honesty and I own our own homes...'

3

One week later

RHYS AND EUNICE ARE STROLLING hand in hand beside a field of wheat, totally oblivious to a group of farm labourers walking on the far side who are pointing at the couple, nudging each other and smirking after the two of them have passed.

Rhys is unmistakable, with his small Welsh harp slung over his shoulder, and Eunice is instantly recognisable – even at a distance – with her striking, raven-black hair.

They walk on, enjoying the sunshine, and eventually settle down to a picnic of bread and cheese, sitting on a woollen blanket and taking in the view across the beautiful valley to the farm nestling in a fold in the hill opposite their vantage point.

'Eunice, I know my father has spoken to you about me taking over the droving and going to London at the end of next week. What do you really feel about that?'

'I feel more worried whenever you use my name like that, when it's just you and me together! Of course I'm concerned that you'll be changed by the experience and that we might be changed for the worse as a result.'

'Me too! But my father's right about the money side of things and he's in poor health these days, actually much, much worse than he admits. I can't let him down. I'll have to go.'

'I know that. I'll be here for you.'

With that, Eunice leans over to him and kisses him tenderly, her green eyes glistening with half-formed tears. She regains her composure in time to stop herself crying.

'Now, seeing as how as you've brought your harp with you, you'd better play it and sing *Idle Days in Summertime* for me.'

Rhys takes up his harp, places it in his lap and, looking at Eunice, begins to sing the song.

Idle days in summertime,
In pleasant sunny weather,
Amid the golden colour'd corn,
Two lovers pass'd together.

Many words they did not speak
To give their thoughts expression,
Each knew the other's heart was full,
But neither made confession!

Winter came, and then, alas!
Came cold and dreary weather;
No more the lovers pass'd their days
Amid the fields together.
Cruel fate had sever'd them,
And both are broken-hearted;
Had they been wed in summertime,
They would not now be parted!

Rhys finishes and looks over to Eunice who is lying on the rug, sobbing.

'Not really the right song for the occasion, is it?'

'Hardly.' Eunice sits up and tries to laugh off her tears.

'I'll only be gone for five weeks or so, if we're lucky with the weather.'

'And everything else.'

'But what can change in that short time?'

'Life turns on an instant. We both know that.'

4

The night before the drove

A CROWDED INN SEES THE drovers and their wives and friends all talking very excitedly at their farewell party. Rhys and Eunice couldn't have been sitting closer together if they'd tried.

A few members of the choir are singing a stirring Welsh march when Drover Jones, sitting next to Caradog, breaks off, jumps up suddenly and taps the table in front of him.

Tall, wiry and silver-haired, with piercing grey eyes, he is immediately the centre of attention.

'Now, we've an early start, to be perfectly honest, and a long and hard few weeks ahead of us.'

Boos nearly drown him out, but he continues.

'So come on, let's call it a day and sing one final song.'

They all stand and sing *Counting the Goats*, getting faster and faster with each chorus until all the words merge together and they sink back into their seats, exhausted.

5

Back to the drove

RHYS GREETS HONESTY JONES WHO is riding across the sand towards him.

'Well done, Rhys. You've led your first crossing.'

'Yes, and only one lost and left behind.'

'Ah, well. There's more than that we've left behind.'

'Still, only one beast lost.'

'And a lot more to lose with every mile we make from now on. Come on, let's get everything together and start in a tidy fashion at least.'

The scene on the seashore is a melee of men, cattle, dogs and horses, with every effort being concentrated on assembling the herd and trying to calm them and settle them after their crossing.

Rhys rides down to the ferryman who is out of his boat and walking towards him.

'Well good luck to you! You'll need it.'

'Don't worry, you'll be seeing us back here in less than two months.'

'Not if I see you first.'

Rhys reaches into his coat and pulls out a sheaf of wheat fashioned into a corn dolly.

'Here, please give this to Eunice for me and tell her to keep it with her at all times until I return.'

'That's a bit sentimental for a drover, isn't it?'

With no time to waste arguing with the gently mocking and smiling ferryman, Rhys heads back up to the head of the herd.

With some of his fellow drovers on horseback and some on foot, they and their fellow travellers wave at the far shore and, to shouts of 'move 'em on, head 'em up', the caravan of people and animals starts the drove.

Corgis are barking at the cattle at the back and yapping at their hind legs to get them moving on up. Border collies keep the sides of the long column of the herd in some kind of shape.

With a final shout of 'move 'em out', they're off.

6

HONESTY, AS THE TOPSMAN, at first rides slightly in front, but now drops back to ride side by side with Rhys. In his head, he runs through the herd and the entourage in general trying to get a fix on numbers and, relying on Rhys's memory to fill in any gaps, tries to make sure that the facts are registered in more than one head.

It is raining hard now and the two men pull their wide-brimmed hats down over their eyes and gather the sacking that they wear as outer cover tightly over their shoulders.

Rhys is glad that, in addition to his wool clothing, he remembered to put the waxed paper, which his father had left out for him, next to his skin. His heavy trousers are already sodden from the seawater.

He regretted only wearing flannel socks and thought he might have to raid the stock of knee-length woollen stockings made in Bala that he had brought with him to sell on the way.

He has his thick-soled boots back on after the crossing, although Honesty now wears long socks and wooden clogs and has already mocked Rhys for his extravagant boots and saddle, made from matching deep-red coloured leather.

They kick on up the slope of the bank.

Both men sit at the same height in the saddle, which is convenient for talk between them – especially with the rain beating in their faces – although Rhys is on his young cob whilst Honesty is on his garron, the type of undersized horse he favours like most other drovers.

'Well, we have four hundred and one head of cattle.'

'Minus one,' Rhys corrects him.

'Yes, of course! We've four corgis and three collies and four ponies.'

'Aren't you going to count the drovers first?'

'Very funny, Rhys! Let's see if you can count and name them if you're so clever.'

'That's easy. You, me, Big Idris, Guto, John Griffiths, Richard Price and William Williams.'

'Who's our farrier?'

'William doubles as that.'

'Who's smuggling the sea salt to sell?'

'What do you mean? Nobody would dare, would they, without telling you?'

'Rhys, you've a lot to learn. Look at Richard Price's saddlebag. It's an expensive one. Leather like yours, but it was around his neck across the Strait and look how he protects it now beneath his outer garments. Vain though you are, you're not doing that.

'He thinks the main enemy against him making his profits is the weather. I've got news for him. The worst threat he faces is me, when I challenge him about what he's doing. He'll have to admit it and concede to sharing his ill-gotten gains with us all. He'll also have to guard it with his life and sleep with that wretched saddlebag under his head.

'He'll have to watch out too for the tricky thieves we'll meet on the road, especially in the inns, most of all their dodgy landlords, who'll be looking out for him. He's well known on this route as Price The Salt.'

'Well here's a tricky question for *you*. How many night watchmen are travelling with us?'

A moment's hesitation only and Honesty replies.

'That's easy, Rhys. Twelve! And they're all wearing the same colour little leather boots as you are, so I know that they are *your* dozen Brecon Buffs by their feet, as well as knowing that your father always sends a gaggle of Roman geese guards on a drove.'

'Who exactly are our travellers? They seem to be keeping themselves to themselves.'

'The younger one is Robert Williams, Sir Hugh Williams's boy – you know, the Member of Parliament for Beaumaris. We do a lot of contract and finance work for him, as well as his droving, and he's asked me to take his youngest son, who's eighteen, down to London where he's going to start his Grand Tour of Europe, would you believe? He will have to get used to being shaken up if he's going to survive that.'

'The other one's also a bit quiet, isn't he?'

'Well he is so far, and with good reason. We know him well. He started out trying to be an animal doctor and went off to a new veterinary college in London. He qualified, God knows how, because when he came back he thought he was going to be more popular than an ordinary doctor, but that didn't turn out to be the case. Certainly people would've seen him as more important if he could cure their animals than if he could cure any human.'

'What happened?'

'Our Doctor was never much good as an animal doctor and his efforts at birthing calves looked more like butchery. So he's since retrained as a sawbones at the local hospital and is now going to join the army or navy, to practise his skills. Nobody knows whether that's going to be as a vet or a doctor, but the joke is that it won't matter which, as his patients there will have already been butchered. To him people and animals are all lambs to the slaughter.'

'So that's the famous doctor. He lives up to his name then, of Doctor Dai-The-Death Davies.'

'I suppose at least he knows what he wants to do, Rhys. What about you? What do you want to make of your life?'

'I like the idea of droving, but I never imagined myself doing it for a living, for the rest of my life. What did you feel when you started?'

'Oh, I saw it as a means to an end, like all work unless you absolutely love it. Trouble is, it's all too easy to forget what the end is. Most people do.'

'And what is it?'

'For me, it's being well and happy and having the time to do what I love doing.'

'Which is?'

'Being at home with my family, free from fear and working on my family farm. And I don't want to make the mistake of only realising what life is all about when I'm too old to enjoy it, to be honest. What about you?'

'Well, it's no secret I like poetry and music and need time for that.'

'That's the point, Rhys, and why your father's so keen that you take over from me. If you could build up the banking side as well as the droving, well, with three or four droves a year, you would be well set financially and free to do what you love doing. How else will it work?'

A shout from one of the drovers causes the two men to slow their pace at the top of the slope. And Honesty turns to look at a red-haired and red-faced Big Idris who runs up alongside.

'The herd's very unsettled. I think we ought to have a stop here and let them catch their breath. They haven't fully recovered from the crossing.'

'Yes, you're right, Idris. Go and bring a couple of corgis to the front and spread the word to the others. Then use that booming voice of yours to call a halt.'

Idris runs back round the side of the herd to carry out his orders whilst Honesty turns to Rhys.

'As you can see, Idris is useful in a great many ways. He's a gentle giant, but despite having immense physical strength, deep down he's just a boy off the farm. He has lived with Welsh Blacks all his life. He's known as the "cowboyo" because his parents even used to make him sleep in the barn with the cattle and, as a result, he can sense their every mood.

'He can't read or write, of course, but he doesn't seem to mind and his loyalty's unwavering. You can trust him with your life. He's saved my bacon more than a few times, I can tell you. He's right to ease our pace – after all, the old saying is go slowly and you'll go far.'

7

By the time the drovers and the yapping corgis bring the herd to a halt, it is clear that Idris had been right. They are spooked and restless.

Rhys looks at the hundred and fifty yards or so of animals, many still snorting and steaming from the exertion of the crossing and the subsequent climb, and marvels at how Idris moves to the front of them and, after only a few moments, when calm is restored, waves his stick in the air and stands aside to get the herd moving on.

The stick had also signalled to the drovers at the rear to get the corgis going again.

Thankfully the rain stops, which helps ease the fretting of the cattle and makes it easier to see what's what and where they're headed.

It's downhill for a while through beautiful countryside. The wide old drovers' road is winding its way ahead as the sun comes out and visibility is restored.

'How good are your eyes, Rhys?'

'Pretty good – I can see when I'm about to be challenged!'

'Right then! Show me where you think we're headed and tell me why.'

Rhys scans the distance and points. 'We're headed that way, way over there. See those three Scots pines on the horizon, maybe four or five miles away? That's a sign that the farmer there will provide food, accommodation and grazing for the night. I'm guessing that's where we're going.'

'I can tell that wily old Caradog has done some schooling of you and you've listened at least. Well then, you'd better make yourself useful and ride ahead to the farm and warn them to get ready for our arrival. That'll show Guto that you're working your passage and know what you're about.'

'I've been meaning to ask you, Honesty – why is he one of our drovers? I thought he wanted to run his own show. He's got a licence and he even touted for our work.'

'He wants it all right. He's even offered me a share of the pickings from any farmers that I can get to use him.'

'So he wants to work on you on this trip?'

'Yes! And at the same time to see what you're made of and if you're going to be the competition. You'd best be on your guard and on your mettle at all times. He'll try and needle you too, I would've thought, to be perfectly honest, so mind how you go.'

8

Rhys rides off at a gentle canter and, taking in the rolling green of the scenery, thinks back to the morning when he left the old farmhouse.

He had been excited all night. Here was a chance, an escape from the routine of his life. An adventure.

Yet, he had felt a growing anxiety too – of leaving Eunice and being separated from the life he knew so well.

He had felt excitement at being able to make his own way as well as worry about doing it on his own. He could feel free from his father's control, but at the same time, cut off from his wisdom and experience. And all alone.

When it had come to the departure, he had been overcome with sadness, of losing his dependence on others. He had had to fight back the tears.

He was still feeling it now and his eyes welled up once more. But, at the same time, came a feeling of new-found independence, of being his own man and making his own way.

With that thought, his confidence returns.

Yes, sure, he knew that every time he had left home in the past, even on a short journey, he had felt the sadness of separation, but he knew that it was not long before that had passed and he had felt guilt that it had given way to a kind of escape euphoria.

He realises, if he's being completely straight with himself, that some of this mixed response had formed part of his feelings at leaving Eunice too, but, with even more guilt at this thought, he decides to shrug it off as a healthy complication that everyone must feel and one that he must try and capture in verse one of these days.

He rides now directly toward the farm, which is only a little way off. He stops and looks back at the herd.

He also sees a group of maybe two or three horsemen, quite separate, a mile or two over to the right and a little way behind the blackness of the cattle. He thinks nothing of it and turns to ride on to the farm.

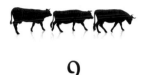

9

HE REACHES THE WHITEWASHED FARMHOUSE AND, riding up its drive, is struck by seeing no animals at all. He hears a few echoey barks, but otherwise nothing.

He rides into the farmyard. Clean, yes. Tidy, certainly. But no animals and no sign of life.

'Hello,' he shouts, 'anybody home?'

The door opens and out comes a ruddy-faced farmer, probably the same age as his own dear father, pointing an old pistol straight at Rhys.

'Who wants to know?'

'My name's Rhys and I'm with Honesty Jones driving a large herd bound for London.'

'Why didn't you say so?'

The farmer turns and hands the gun to his wife who has appeared behind him at the door. He turns back to face Rhys.

'Well, I'm Arfon Protheroe and this is my wife, Angharad. You must be Caradog's son. We were told to expect you sometime, but we didn't know it would be so soon.'

Rhys senses the woman staring at him intently.

'You came once before, didn't you? How is your father and what news from your part of the world?'

'There'll be plenty of time for that later, Angharad. We must get on with preparations. You go back to the kitchen and make a start on the cawl. Have we enough bread?'

'Yes, ever since you said to expect Honesty, I've been baking all week and getting things ready.'

With that, the farmer's wife goes back into the farmhouse and Rhys dismounts, to talk to the farmer on an even footing.

'How big's the drive?'

'Four hundred cattle, twelve geese, seven dogs, five ponies and seven drovers. And two travellers with their own ponies: a doctor returning to London and a young squire off on the start of his Grand Tour.'

'Well, you've a fair memory, I'll give you that. You can have Halfpenny Field, which is the one to the left as you come in at the bottom of the drive. I hardly need to tell you that it's a halfpenny a head per night.'

'For the cattle?'

'Of course for the cattle, you young fool.'

'Well, how much is that?'

'I hope you aren't being serious, Rhys. You know your 3Rs – you should've worked out the answer for yourself. How else will you know whether you're being taken advantage of? You'd better brush up on your arithmetic before Honesty finds out.'

'Just testing! The answer is sixteen shillings and eight pennies. What's the rate for the rest of us and our animals?'

'That's threepence a night per person, including food – cheaper than any inn, mind. Oh and plus a few more pence for hay for the animals and some food for the dogs.'

'I've been told to barter for a good price.'

'Well, that isn't the way to start a negotiation. You're already now at a disadvantage. Anyway, be that as it may, and it may well be, tell me what you propose.'

'Well, as this is a large herd, what about half price?'

'A farthing? Why, I'd then have to rename it Farthing Field, wouldn't I? No chance! I tell you what. For your father's sake and to save you face with Honesty, I'll round it down to sixteen shillings for the cattle. How is that?'

'Thank you. It's a deal. A reduction of one twenty-fifth. How is that for arithmetic?'

'You crafty so-and-so. You'll make a drover yet.'

'By the way, where do we sleep?'

'Four people can go in the house and the rest in this nearest barn as I've got some livestock and a couple of my dogs in the far barn. You'll have to work out for yourselves which of you is on watch and who sleeps where. I take it your travellers'll pay the sixpence each for themselves and their ponies so they'd better be in the house rather than in the barn.

'There's also an old stone-built shepherd's hut at the corner of Halfpenny Field. A couple of drovers usually sleep there and take it in turns to keep watch with one or two of the dogs. Your father always used to keep the geese in with the cattle.'

'Nothing ever happens though, does it?'

'You'd be surprised, the stories the drovers tell. Also, I heard from my neighbours over the hill that there were some rustlers operating not that far away from here recently and I heard that the Jones brothers are back to their old ways. A few days ago, a stranger even called in here to ask when the next drive was coming through. Of course, I told him nothing.'

'I'd better be getting back to the herd to help bring them in. See you later.'

'I look forward to it. Honesty is a great favourite with us and we'll have an enjoyable evening. We might even tempt you to play that small harp of yours I can see strapped to your pony. You can treat us to a tune or two and give us a chance to judge for ourselves whether you're as good as people say you are.'

Rhys, slightly flushed, hurriedly mounts up and, with a wave of his hand, rides off to rejoin the others.

10

THE DRIVE IS GOING WELL by the time he rejoins it and it looks well organised until he's close up, when he sees that it's a strain to keep the herd under control and the animals themselves look ready to run in every direction if they're ever given the chance.

'A good welcome awaits us, I hope?'

This is an opening gambit from Guto, who follows up with, 'And I trust you got us as good a rate as I would've got, given half a chance.'

'Leave the money side to me, Guto,' chips in Honesty, riding up to get the report from Rhys.

Guto rides off around the side, tutting to himself, shaking his head and wiping his mouth and bearded face with the back of his hand.

He is tense and annoyed, that's for sure, and he flashes Rhys a backwards, hostile look. Honesty sees it too.

'It doesn't take long for the resentment to come out with Guto, but just try and ignore it and not rise to his ribbing. Anyway, how's it looking for tonight?'

Rhys fills in the details, but he also mentions what he'd been told about rustlers, the wild Jones brothers and the fact that he had seen some horsemen in the distance himself. Honesty looks unmoved by this development.

'Nothing will happen hereabouts, but we'd do well to keep a sharp eye and maybe do some scouting when we get into the hills. Some of the passes are ideal spots for an ambush.'

'I'd tell the drovers who keep watch tonight to be extra vigilant too.'

'Well, if I asked you to do that for me, Rhys, you would be talking to yourself because you'll be doing a stretch on watch tonight.'

It's not long before they arrive at the farm and the gate to Halfpenny Field is open ready for them, opened outwards to block the entrance to the drive up to the farm.

Before they know it, all the cattle and geese are in the field and all the men and animals are quartered in the barn and in the house.

Night falls quickly and they sit down in turn to be fed and watered. Two men volunteer to do the first watch and so it's Guto and Richard Price who head off to do their stint, having eaten quickly whilst Honesty and Idris were out with a couple of the dogs, looking over the herd.

They had seemed pleased when they had returned with how the animals had settled, grazing the lush grass and drinking noisily from the water troughs happily enough.

'What will those two be plotting?' Rhys wants to know, as Guto and Richard leave and, he adds, 'Have you noticed that Guto looks right through you while Richard never looks anyone straight in the eye – what a pair,' but he receives only a shrug from Honesty for his pains.

The mood becomes more relaxed. The Doctor and the young gentleman soon retire to their room complaining of being saddle-sore, to much merriment from the others.

Honesty is prevailed upon to give his famous recitation. After the food plates are cleared away, he stands and, taking a flower from the vase on the dresser, puts it in his buttonhole and starts up. He acts out every line of this dramatic monologue, his party piece:

My name is Tomas Tomas from Pen Llandeilo'r-Fan
My brother's name is William and my sister's name is Siân
And whenever I go courtin' in weather cold or hot,
I have round my neck a muffler and a posy in my co't

I was cross the side of Epynt for sweet Nancy Price to see,
For to ask her to go to November Fair with me.

She said 'yes' and on that morning what
a lovely shawl she got,
I had round my neck a muffler and a posy in my co't.

I was take her to the waxworks and the Market Hall to see,
On swingboats I did shiggle her and she did shiggle me.
On horses made of sticks we did gallop round and round
And a gipsy played the fiddle in the middle of the ground.

Then we went to coffee tavern for some sausages and tart,
When a gentleman came over, smoked cigar, looked so smart
And said: 'Excuse me squire, what a lovely flower you got!'

I was glad he called me squire — made me high before the lot,
So I was gladly let him smell the lovely posy in my co't.
Then to pay for tart and sausage, on the waiter I did call,
Searched my pockets for some money,
Trousers, waistco't, co't and all and I hollered,
'Someone's robbed me, there's pickpockets in this lot!'

I was breathing very fast and was red and very hot
Someone shouted, 'who asked to smell the posy
Tomas Tomas in your co't?'

I was tear my hair in fistfuls
I was kick the coffee pot
And I tore in a hundred pieces that old posy in my co't.

Sweet Nancy Price said, 'stop your crying Tomas Tomas
Dry your eyes and wipe your nose.
I have money, two and sixpence,
Hear them jingle in my clothes'.

Honesty acknowledges the applause. The farmer asks for a song from Rhys, but Honesty waves his hand, saying that that will have to await the return journey and, sensing that everyone is ready to retire, he gives instructions for the night ahead.

'Right, well you all know where you're sleeping. Rhys and William, you need to go out later and relieve Guto and Richard.'

'How will I be sure to wake?'

'Don't worry, Rhys, William has his internal drover's clock and I have mine, so we'll make sure you're awake'.

In the hallway, Arfon Protheroe takes Honesty aside and voices, in a half whisper, a concern that has been building up in his mind.

'Look, this may be something and nothing, but I mentioned to Rhys when he arrived here today that a stranger had called earlier in the week to ask when the next big drive was coming through. I told him I didn't know, but it's been nagging away at me ever since. I'd forgotten until just now that he'd also asked me what route you drovers usually take after your stopover here.'

'Well, what did you say to that?'

'I lied, I'm afraid. I said that I didn't always know for sure, but thought they went north east.'

'What made you say that? We never do that unless the weather is coming in really bad. Sounds to me like he may just be scouting out the route for another droving outfit.'

'I don't think so. There was something about him made me suspicious. I didn't like the cut of his jib. I didn't know why at the time, but I've just had a flash. I think he's one of the Jones brothers. You know, the one who went off to prison in Ruthin several years back. He's got a beard now, but his face fits the family features all right.'

'Thanks, Arfon. I'll think on that, but I won't tell you what we're going to do in case they come back to question you. Best you know nothing. You'd better take care yourself.'

Honesty and Arfon are pushed out of the way by the others, anxious to try and get as many hours' sleep as they can. They all go their separate ways and it's not long before the house and the barn are settled and quiet.

Meanwhile, at Halfpenny Field, Guto has strolled around the perimeter with one of the collies who seems mightily agitated at something.

It causes Guto to keep looking about him in a panicky way as if being attacked by a silent wasp and he thanks his lucky stars that it's a clear night with plenty of moonlight. He sees nothing unusual even if every dark shape seems sinister and threatening.

He's uneasy when he returns to the hut and more than slightly disappointed to find Richard fast asleep.

Richard grunts when he receives a gentle kick from Guto and sits up.

'What was that for?'

'For a start, we're on watch. What if we both dozed off?'

'Well we didn't, did we? I knew you were out there.'

'Yes, but what if I'd called you?'

'Guto, your voice could raise the dead. What's got into you?'

'Somebody is out there. I know it. The dog knows it. Look, he's still totally on edge.'

They both jump with a start when the geese loudly cackle all together as if bang on cue. The dog barks. The cattle bellow.

'Someone's out there. Come on and bring your stick.'

They both run out and shout, 'Who's there? We know you're out there.'

They walk quickly around the field and can see nothing. The dog makes to chase something moving and, suddenly, they see a large fox picking up speed down the driveway.

The two men look at each other and laugh.

'Spooked by a fox. We'd better keep quiet about this, otherwise we won't hear the last of it.'

'Don't tell Rhys and William when they take over. And if there is anything else out there, we don't want to spoil their fun, do we?'

'Ah, Rhys. What do you make of him, Guto?'

'Well he's had it easy, hasn't he. His father spoils him and Honesty treats him like he's his own son. They can't see how soft he is. Let him do his singing, I say. It's all he's good for.'

'Am I right in thinking you're a bit jealous, Guto?'

'Don't be daft. Jealous of what?'

'Well, I know you were also sweet on his Eunice once.'

'No I wasn't.'

'Are you blushing, Guto?'

'Don't be ridiculous. Anyhow, you can't possibly tell that in this light.'

They then take it in turns to keep an eye on the herd and have no more scares until they hear footsteps approaching and are mightily glad to hear William's whispered 'Wake up you two' as he and Rhys walk into the hut.

'We are awake,' they reply together.

'Anything to report?'

'Nothing so far, but keep an eye out for rustlers, gentlemen,' says Guto, 'they've been about in this area and they usually come in the middle of the night.'

Richard picks up his precious saddlebag and he and Guto head off back to the farm. They are walking quickly, anxiously looking all around them the whole time.

PART TWO

11

A few days later

GUTO RIDES UP TO HONESTY and is clearly angry.

'Why we've had to come this way I just don't understand. If we'd wanted to take the higher ground, we should've gone the coastal way.'

'I have my reasons, Guto.'

'Such as what? We've a right to know. The weather's been grim. You first headed south from Protheroe's as usual and then, for some reason, you made us take the old way which heads to the Moors.'

'It'll be quicker.'

'Only if the weather doesn't worsen. And Idris worries that the cattle will come through the worse for wear.'

'Well, so far, so good.'

'That's not the point.'

'Guto, I don't want to alarm you all, to be honest, especially our travellers, but I think the Jones brothers are after us and I wanted to put them off our trail.'

'What? And you didn't think to tell us?'

'I'm only doing so now because I have to. I think I've sighted them a mile or two back.'

'We'll have to tell the men.'

'Yes, all right. Go and fetch Rhys and William. We will take a stop now and try and hatch a plan. I've had plenty of time to think of one.'

Idris is signalled to stop the herd and Guto rides round to tell the men and the travellers the reason for the interruption to the day's drive.

Honesty outlines the facts to Rhys, William and Guto, with Guto chipping in colour and atmosphere – mainly swearing about the violent ways of the Jones brothers.

'Up ahead,' explains Honesty, 'the old road runs between a wood on one side and a stone wall on the other, higher side. That's where we'll lay our trap. There's a place for the herd to be corralled just beyond and that means it's the perfect spot to make our stand.'

As he outlines his plan, the three men throw in doubts as well as support and eventually they disperse to share the dangers with the others.

Guto rides back to the front.

'They all know what they have to do and are ready for it. We've not many weapons between us, so I'm not hopeful of the outcome.'

'Defeatism, you know, as an approach to life, Guto, just doesn't work.'

The herd is taken ahead, through the narrowing of the road between the wood and the wall as described by Honesty, to an old enclosed field into which the cattle are driven, the better to be safer from stampeding when the noise of the expected encounter gets underway.

The travellers are put on herding duties as that is simple enough for them. They have to guard the ungated entrance to the field to keep the cattle enclosed.

Back down the road, but within sight of the herd, Honesty and Rhys wait on horseback, with the others positioned, hidden, in the wood and the other ponies tethered deeper into it.

Idris is behind the wall at the top of the bank on the higher side of the road, where a small stone platform has been hastily constructed and which he now crouches beside, completely obscured from view.

The wait is short and riding up fast behind them are three men. As planned, Honesty and Rhys turn their ponies towards the sound of the clattering hooves and Honesty holds up a hand.

The three strangers come to a halt ten yards from them, but slowly edge closer.

'Well, well, well. Honesty himself. So honest that he sticks out like a sore thumb in our family.'

'Rhodri. How nice of you to come and see me. And you only just out of prison.'

'Why wouldn't I, when you've such a nice big herd. I would've been here earlier, but you've led us quite a dance changing direction like that. We waited for you north east of old Protheroe's place. Are you sure you know what you're doing? You're a bit too old for this sort of thing, aren't you? You can't seem to find your way and you never know who you're going to meet, do you?'

'Cut the cackle, Rhodri. What do you want?'

'I'm going to make it easy for you. I want the money you're carrying. Not just yours, mind. I also want the money and valuables that your two travelling gents have. We've seen them. We've been watching you for a while now, haven't we boys?'

Rhodri turns to his two brothers who now take out their guns and the youngest, Gruf Rhys, nervously strokes the side of his stubbled face with the barrel of his and then gestures toward the herd with it.

'Very good of you to pick a spot right out in the middle of nowhere to stop and have a rest.'

'Yes indeed,' joins in Rhodri. 'Give us what we ask for, no bother, and we won't even stampede the herd.'

'And then we won't have to kill you, which we will if we have to, even though you're our cousin,' adds the middle brother Aneurin, jerking his head anxiously as his face visibly develops a severe twitch.

'This is utter madness. You'll never get away with it.'

'Says who?'

'I'm Rhys Morgan. Son of Caradog.'

'And what'll you do? Get your harp out and hit me with it?'

Rhodri is pleased with his reply and his brothers laugh loudly as if it is the wittiest remark they have ever heard, which it probably is.

Honesty, after a lifetime of standing up to bullies, angrily silences the brothers. 'You're a disgrace to your parents.'

This works to incense Rhodri who takes out his pistol and waves it at Honesty.

'It's time to wipe that smug self-satisfied smile off your face permanently.'

'Not so fast,' booms out a voice from behind the wall.

The brothers all turn to look. Big Idris stands on the stone platform and towers over the wall that itself looks vast from down below. High above his head, he holds a large stone and hurls it ferociously at Rhodri, who is sitting stock-still in amazement at seeing an apparent giant looming above him.

Rhodri's knocked clean off his horse. Then Guto and William leap out from behind the trees holding their pistols.

Gruf Rhys takes aim at Honesty, but is beaten to the shot by Honesty himself who fires his pistol at Gruf Rhys's shoulder.

The force of the blast sends the young Jones brother off his horse. Aneurin quickly drops his pistol, puts his hands up and shouts, 'OK, OK, don't shoot.'

Idris jumps over the wall and runs up the road to the herd, which is so agitated by the sound of the gunshot that he can see the travellers in danger of being forced to abandon their post.

Guto and William step out of the wood to disarm Rhodri, who is still stunned from his fall and sways as he gets to his feet. Gruf Rhys, who is writhing in agony on the floor, shouts, 'Help, I've been shot. I've been shot.'

John and Richard run from their cover to take the reins of the Jones brothers' ponies to prevent them taking off.

Honesty shouts to make himself heard above the din.

'Rhodri. This is a wake-up call to you. I'm going to let you go this time.'

Guto is outraged.

'Bloody hell. You can't do that. What message does that give out? They deserve to die for this.'

'I haven't finished yet, Guto. Hear me out. We're better than that. Rhodri, you and your brothers are finished here. We're taking your weapons, of course, but you can keep your ponies. If you know what's good for you, you'll ride them to Liverpool and sell them to pay your passage to

America. You might have more luck over there. If you ever return to North Wales, I'll have you arrested. And you'll all hang, as thieves, rustlers and highwaymen. I'll make a full report to the magistrate on our return from London. Now, patch your brother up and all of you get out of my sight.'

12

AFTER ALL THIS EXCITEMENT, the afternoon is a relatively relaxed time. The drovers go round each other to discuss the ins and outs of their ordeal and review each other's performances, almost leaving the dogs to drive the cattle on their own.

Needless to say, Honesty and Idris see their stock rise in the eyes of the men, but Rhys realises that he'll probably never shake off the 'hit me with your harp' line.

After Guto has bent his ear about the folly of Honesty letting the Jones brothers go, Rhys is glad to be alone with his thoughts as he rides alongside the herd, occasionally shouting at strays and making sure they get back into line.

All around him, the countryside soothes with its green and vibrant beauty and the noise of the cattle, the barking of the dogs and the shouts of the men do little to disturb his reverie.

Even with its dangers, the freedom of this life on the road suddenly appeals to him. Honesty's knowledge of the green drovers' roads has filled him with the desire to know more; not just on how to avoid the toll roads, but how the wide open spaces can broaden your mind.

His protected home life has been too restrictive, he decides. He needs to get out of his valley of safety and up over the hills to see the opportunities more clearly.

Rhys ponders what they might be, but before he can identify them he hears the shout of the front men warning an upcoming hamlet and its farmers that a large herd is coming through. This warns them to lock up their animals to prevent them joining the herd and, no doubt, protect their womenfolk too from the rough 'animals' who are driving it through.

All the men and the travellers are looking forward to this evening when they are due to stop at one of the drovers' inns that Honesty has excited them all about and that Rhys himself remembers from his boyhood trip. They all know that they will have food and drink and company aplenty as well as the chance to take it easy, knowing the herd is confined to a field where keeping an eye on them is a simpler operation.

Honesty catches up with Rhys whose pace has slowed.

'Come on, Rhys, look alive, we're all outpacing you, even Idris here, and he's on foot at that.'

'Sorry, I was miles away.'

'Wishing you were, no doubt.'

'Hardly. What with the excitement of the Jones brothers and the prospect of tonight, I'm getting into all this.'

'Well, here's something else to learn. Idris has been telling me some of the cattle are needing shod. So tomorrow, early, so as not to delay our start, you can give Guto and William a hand at all that. Idris will pick out the cows concerned and then Guto, who is our thrower, will get them ready for William to do his farrier duties.'

'What does a thrower have to do? I already know that Guto can throw a good insult, but what's it mean for the cattle?'

Idris raises his eyebrows – as Honesty explains that the thrower's job is to wrestle a cow to the ground so that it can be shod – and then he protectively adds his advice.

'Rhys, whatever you do, don't let Guto challenge you to having a go. You're bull-headed enough to rise to the challenge, but it takes massive strength and years of practice to do it. You can help me rope the cows as I spot them out to you.

'And Idris is right. You'll have to learn how to handle Guto. Anyway, make yourself useful now. Ride ahead and get our lodgings sorted out.'

Rhys does not need telling twice and rides off on what he has seen as a perk of his position. Only now, is he dimly beginning to see it as being some kind of comment on all he is fit for.

Through the mixed purples and yellows of the heather and gorse, the green lane winds around natural obstacles and is occasionally crossed by fast-flowing streams. The cattle will have no trouble with these after the Menai Strait, he thinks, but it'll slow things down as they stop to drink.

He knows that he has an hour or two to himself and slows his pace accordingly. He daydreams as he rides and loses track of time until he sees a wooded area just ahead and, recognising it as an ash grove, sings a favourite song in loud and lusty fashion, startling a young doe in the process that bounds away fast, by way of critical comment.

The ash grove how graceful how plainly 'tis speaking,
The harp thro' it playing has language for me;
Whenever the light thro' its branches is breaking,
A host of kind faces is gazing on me.
The friends of my childhood again are before me,
Each step wakes a mem'ry as freely I roam,
With soft whispers laden, its leaves rustle o'er me,
The ash grove, the ash grove alone is my home.
My lips smile no more, my heart loses its lightness,
No dream of the future my spirit can cheer,
I only would brood on the past and its brightness,

The dead I have mourn'd are again living here.
From ev'ry dark nook they press forward to meet me,
I lift up my eyes to the broad leafy dome,
And others are there looking downwards to greet me,
The ash grove, the ash grove alone is my home.

Emerging into the sunlight from the trees, Rhys shudders slightly, uplifted yet depressed by his rousing rendition of a song whose meaning, until that moment, had not really been clear to him.

Fortunately, just as he is beginning to think fondly of home and his life there, he sees that the road is sloping gently downhill and there, below him in the valley, is their next stop.

13

RIDING INTO THE SMALL VILLAGE and passing only a few cottages, Rhys rides to the crossroads and heads away from one old inn at the junction and towards the rival inn slightly further on, the one favoured by Honesty all these years.

He's not sure, purely on visual evidence, that they're choosing the right one, as he passes an attractive, comfortable, thatched hostelry and heads on over to a far less salubrious one that already seems to have quite a few travellers in residence, to judge by the horses outside and the noise of revelry coming from within, despite it still being the afternoon.

And yet Honesty knows best, he thinks, and anyway, this is the drovers' inn and they do have the large fields to the rear for the cattle, so that's that.

He dismounts and ties his pony to the iron ring set in the wall at the front of the inn and, feeling slightly sore, walks stiffly through the front door and into a crowded bar area.

Silence descends as he enters and all the faces turn to his. As if this isn't daunting enough, the burly landlord shouts across to him from behind the wooden counter, 'Where's my friend Guto? I thought he was going to be running this drive.'

'He's with the herd. And, actually, it's Honesty's drive.'

Groans greet this and he hears mumbles of 'it'll be best behaviour then' and 'no swearing you lot or you'll have the wrath of the Lord God Honesty Jones down on you'.

'Prices are up this year,' the landlord booms, looking smugly around his customers, as Rhys stops and looks him in the eye. 'And we'll want payment up front.'

The packed room is in silence again as Rhys leans on the bar and looks slowly round. He notices a group of rather swarthy individuals in prime position by the smoky log fire and takes in that they are studying him particularly intently.

'No! We'll pay what we paid last year and not a penny more.'

'Well, I can't remember what that was, so I'll give you the current rate.'

'No need, landlord. I have the books of account here and can tell you to the last halfpenny what we spent with you. I can ride back and tell Honesty to travel on or try elsewhere if you like, or I can tell him you'll agree last year's rates. Your choice.'

'Oh well, seeing as it's Honesty. Same rates then.'

The landlord, becoming aware that he is losing face, suddenly hardens his attitude.

'But it will have to be cash up front.'

Sensing the man needs a small victory, Rhys shrugs in answer, 'I'll leave that to you and Honesty.'

Then, from the far corner away from the fire, an old tinker, with his tray of pots and pans in front of him, pipes up, having heard every word of the exchange:

> *Owen Moore went away*
> *Owing more than he could pay.*
> *Owen Moore came back next day.*
> *Owing More.*

'Never mind him,' says the landlord, grateful for Rhys's gesture, 'have a drink on the house before you get off.'

'Thanks for the offer, but I'll water my horse at the trough out front and then be off straight away. We'll be back later. I take it the usual accommodation is available? You seem to have a full house.'

'None are staying here. Most are locals and the rest have lodgings elsewhere, nearer their work on the roads and canals.'

Rhys walks out of the inn and into the fresh air, glad to distance himself from the strange atmosphere, especially as he has a sense of foreboding about it all. He looks back to see that the unpleasant-looking group of inmates is studying him through the window and this does nothing to ease his mood.

He rides back to the herd, anxious to tell Honesty about his encounter, but when he arrives he gets short shrift.

Clearly something has annoyed Honesty, as his reaction is to tell Rhys impatiently not to be so melodramatic and that, if he feels like that now, God knows what he's going to make of places closer to London and in London itself.

Embarrassed and humbled, Rhys retreats to the back and chats to Idris about the whole process of shoeing cattle, which he knows he'll be involved with in the morning.

Honesty knows the inn well and following his instructions and with the usual noise and shouts, the animals are driven into the large field behind the main building.

Most of the occupants turn out to welcome them and it's a large throng that makes its way back inside, where the fire belches even more smoke into the already fuggy room.

14

Rhys notices that Honesty calls the landlord to one side and they both go up the stairs to view the bedrooms. Rhys realises what is going on as it dawns on him that Honesty is showing him the best way to negotiate – away from onlookers who would otherwise be influencing the conversation and therefore the deal.

Indeed, Honesty soon returns with a smile on his face and, following him back down the stairs, is a very sullen and browbeaten landlord.

Downstairs, everyone is still milling around and making their way back into the bar.

Across from the fire and near the door, the drovers find a table and they each sit down at the nearest available chair. Two of them have stayed with the herd, Idris and John – the quiet pair whether in, or out of, an inn.

The rough-looking lot sitting at the table in the corner by the fire take it in turns to glare at the drovers, envious of their status with all the locals and furious the landlord is fussing around them, listening to their news and taking their orders for food and drink.

'What about a bit of service over here for your regulars, landlord?' shouts a large burly beard on legs.

'All in good time. All in good time, fellas. I'm on my way.'

Further annoyed that the attractive landlady has stayed with the drovers, the scowls from the corner are beginning to create a rather aggressive atmosphere, which Honesty, with his sensitivities to such things, picks up on immediately.

The evening proceeds with the drovers beginning to relax. They know their rota for the night and which of them have to sleep outside with the herd. Guto and Richard shift their ale swiftly and take some bread and cheese out with them to go and relieve Idris and John.

Whilst they are getting ready to go, bowls of soup are brought for the drovers and the travellers. Just as they are sharing out the bread and are about to tuck into their food, the corner group, making their way over to the bar, stop by the drovers' table.

The large, heavily built leader of the pack stands behind Honesty's chair, leans over him to pick up his ale and pours most of it into the still-seated Honesty's soup.

'There, that should improve the taste of it for you nicely, you puffed-up cowhand.'

Silence descends. All eyes are on Honesty, wondering what on earth he will do next.

He puts a spoon to the soup, raises it to his mouth and slurps it noisily. Smacking his lips as if testing the taste he then, slowly and with great deliberation, pours the rest of his tankard of ale into the soup.

'That should now give me the full taste it needs, eh lads?'

With that and with the distraction of the laughter it causes, Honesty, in one smooth, rapid movement, stands, turns and punches the tankard he is still holding upwards and into the jaw of his tormentor, a blow that knocks his victim backwards.

All hell is then let loose as the drovers spring to their feet and fight for all they're worth. Both groups are hard at it even in the restricted area and tables and chairs are sent flying.

Eventually, the big, bearded beast gets Honesty in a headlock and yells, 'Stop! One more move by anyone and I'll break his neck.'

Everybody stops and, having their attention, Honesty hoarsely struggles to make himself heard.

'You lot have been spoiling for a fight since we arrived. Let me go or there'll be big trouble.'

'Who do you think you are? Wearing a droving licence on your arm doesn't make you the law around here. I want you outside where we can settle this man to man, once and for all.

Having had quite enough of this, Rhys does the one thing he can think of against a brute of a man who is twice his physical bulk.

He hits him with his harp. Hard. On the back of his head.

With their leader flat out on the floor, the others are quickly overpowered by the drovers. They and the regulars then throw them unceremoniously outside, much to the relief of the landlord.

'We've wanted to do that for weeks – they've been making our lives a misery.'

At this point, Guto, having heard the commotion, runs past the ejected group and its still-dazed ringleader and enters the inn to be told what has happened.

He is astounded to hear that Rhys is the hero of the hour.

'What did he do? Hit him with his harp?'

'Yes, he did actually,' they all respond with one voice and the whole place erupts in laughter.

15

THE MOOD LIFTS AT THAT exchange and one and all set to and restore order to the chaos, righting chairs and tables and getting them back into position.

The landlord fears that he might lose his clientele far too early and so he suggests to Honesty that he and his fellow drovers put on a musical party.

'There's free ale to all performers,' he announces by way of incentive.

'Very well, landlord,' Honesty announces to the crowded bar, 'we will do a few monologues and then Rhys can lead us off with some old songs when you can all join in – that should qualify you all for a free ale.'

'Wait a minute, hang on, calm down. That's not the offer. Free ale only for soloists,' chimes in the landlord.

'Worth a try, eh, lads?'

Honesty was in his element now and playing to his audience.

'First of all, I want to ask Guto to strap on his six shooters and go out and make sure our friends are on their way and won't come back.'

Guto reaches into his saddlebag and pulls out his six guns. He turns this ritual into a performance.

He makes a great ceremony of putting two flintlock pistols with two-inch barrels down, side by side, in front of him on the table. Then he pulls out two pistols with three-inch barrels and places each one outside the first two. Finally, with a great flourish, he reveals two long, four-inch barrelled pistols which go to form the outside frame to the other four.

Everyone closes in on the table as Guto loads the six pistols and places them firmly into his belt, three on each side of his buckle, the smaller ones to the front and the large ones in line with his hips.

'These, gentlemen, are to protect the herd from wolves and to protect us drovers from highwaymen and ne'er do wells.'

To gasps, Guto spins round and swiftly draws the larger weapons so they are in each hand in a trice and pointing straight ahead. People duck and dive to get out of the line of fire.

'Fear not, friends,' Guto shouts, now playing to the gallery and raising his voice in order to strike fear into the men outside as well, 'these guns are used only to kill wild animals and robbers. The faster you can draw, the longer you'll live.'

With that he puts his broad-brimmed felt hat onto his head and walks out to the front of the inn. All those who remain inside rush to the windows, jostling for a view outside.

Once outside, Guto confronts the recently ejected men and the still-dazed bear of a man that they all sheepishly follow as their leader.

'I'll give you twopenny-halfpenny no-good boyos to the count of ten to get your backsides off this property, otherwise I'll pump you full of lead. And don't come back or you'll have me to answer to.'

Guto then, in a flash, draws his two big guns and aims them at his foes.

The bewildered men need no further words of encouragement to leave. Helping their battered and bruised big boss man, they scarper as fast as they can.

16

THE MOOD IS MUCH MORE convivial when Guto makes his way back inside, having waited for a few minutes to watch the men half run, half stumble away into the distance, ill lit by moonlight.

Honesty has already taken up his role as chairman of the proceedings and introduces the quiet man John Griffiths to the assembly.

'John Griffiths is a man of few words and even fewer teeth, so it's a great privilege to ask him to perform his famous monologue of *The Blowing Out of the Candle* for which he is well known throughout the land.'

John steps forward and takes up a seat at the front of the audience with a lit candle – which both lights the performer and doubles as a stage prop – on the table in front of him.

He cuts a strange figure – prematurely grey, hunched and aged, a look exaggerated both by his solitary front tooth and by his unnerving ability to look cross-eyed from time to time at the expectant throng in front of him.

He speaks quietly and yet easily holds the attention required for the delivery of his monologue and its accompanying mime, full of lively actions and facial contortions.

'In an old inn, somewhere in the middle of wild Wales, five old drovers reach the end of a long night's drinking and make ready for to go to bed. Taking a lighted candle from the bar, the head drover leads his men up the stairs to their quarters where he places the candle on the round table in the middle of their room.

'As they are making ready to get into their beds, the head drover, who speaks out of the left side of his mouth, tries to blow out the candle... and fails.

'He calls to the second drover, who speaks out of the right side of his mouth, who also tries to blow out the candle... and fails.

'He calls to the third drover, who has a protruding top lip. He blows boldly at the candle, but the air is blown downwards and the candle stays lit.

'He calls for the fourth drover, who has a protruding bottom lip. He blows upwards and, again, fails to put out the candle.

'They all then call for the fifth drover, who is cross-eyed and has one tooth in the middle of his mouth. Just like me.'

John sits and stares cross-eyed at the candle and then bends slowly forward towards it, as if going to blow it out. Staring ahead with his mad eyes, he purses his lips, but then, just as he is about to blow, he puts out his right hand... and snuffs out the flame between his finger and thumb.

Laughter and applause greet the miming skills of John the quiet storyteller, who then eagerly grasps at the tankard of free ale brought to him for his pains by a smiling landlord.

A couple of the locals, keen to win their free ale, then step forward to sing a duet. The taller of the two introduces himself and his friend to the drovers, as all the other locals heckle them good-naturedly.

'We're local farmers and we're going to sing a duet for you tonight, a favourite song of Henry V when he was Prince of Wales. As a matter of actual fact, it was sung by him and his companions at the Boar's Head Tavern, Cheapside. There's knowledge for you. The song is called *Once a Farmer and his Wife*. Some parts we will sing together but I will sing the farmer and Iorweth here will sing my wife.'

Cue loud cheers and laughter all round.

A couple of stamps of their feet to get the timing and they start up.

Once a farmer and his wife
Had cause for disputation,
They were used to noisy strife,
And wordy altercation;
'Good man,' said she, 'you are too free,
And too open-handed.'
'Good wife,' said he, 'you let me be,
I will not be commanded!'

Then when harvest time came round,
And boys with girls were racing,
Oft the farmer's wife had found
He would the girls be chasing.
'Good man,' cried she, 'you are too free,
And too open-hearted.'
'Good wife,' said he, 'you let me be,
Or we will soon be parted.'

Long, long years did pass away,
And still they kept on railing;
Till at last, one winter's day,

She said, when she was ailing,
'I am too old always to scold,
I think your ways are mended.'
Said he, 'You're right, good wife, quite right,'
And so the matter ended.

The drovers join with the locals in giving a rousing cheer to the singing farmers, who quickly grab the offered tankards and slurp happily at their ale.

Honesty steps forward and holds up his left hand for silence.

'And now, it is my great pleasure to bring you, all the way from Anglesey, the Bard of Beaumaris himself, Rhys Morgan with his famous harp. If we are quiet for him, I am sure he will play it for us this time and not hit us with it. Rhys, what are you going to sing for us tonight?'

Rhys steps forward to perform and introduces himself.

'Tonight, Honesty, I am going to sing for you…'

His performance is stopped before it has started by the crash of the breaking glass of the window at the front of the inn. This is immediately followed by the small explosion of an oil lamp, which has been thrown through the window and bursts into flames.

The main victim, suffering immediate burning to the back of both his hands that he throws up to protect his face, is the young gentleman, Robert Williams, and he screams out in agony. Doctor Dai springs into action and pushes his patient towards the door.

'We've got to get you to the water pump outside straight away.'

There is pandemonium, with the landlord calling for buckets of water to put out the fire inside the inn. Men are jumping up and down on the flames near the exploded lamp. With this and the ale thrown by some onto the flames, the small fire is dampened and finally extinguished by buckets of water arriving from outside.

Honesty and Guto had rushed outside as soon as the window was smashed, but only in time to see three men running down the lane at a very fast lick.

'The guilty flee, Guto, with no one chasing them.'

'No prizes for guessing who they are, the filthy cowards,' snarls Guto, but Honesty had already turned to run towards the herd, which had been disturbed by the noise that had set the dogs off.

Idris had beaten him to it and was already soothing the older cattle that he had placed at the edge of the herd.

'Have we got a problem, Idris?'

'No, they'll be fine. We'll quieten the dogs and that should calm things down a bit.'

'Well done. I'll go back and check on the damage inside.'

By this time all the drovers are out, walking around and talking soothingly to the animals.

Rhys is out at the front by the pump with Doctor Dai as Honesty strolls up.

'How is he, Doc?'

'Well, I won't be amputating, that's for sure.'

'You sound disappointed.'

He asks Rhys to take over pumping the water onto Robert's very sore-looking hands.

'That could have been a whole lot worse if he hadn't covered his face.'

Honesty inspects the hands and tells Rhys to go and fetch their medical bag. The Doctor bridles.

'I can handle this.'

'I am sure you can, but this young man is my responsibility and we know what to do. I'll be letting one of the dogs lick his hands to help heal him over the next few days.'

'Are you mad. You aren't qualified to know what to do.'

'No, that's quite true, but I have a lifetime's experience. I'll be using lard, mutton tallow, beeswax and a few other things too, so the burns can heal and leave very little scarring.'

Doctor Dai looks daggers at Honesty but lets it go as he has already turned away and is walking back into the inn. There he's greeted with the sight of the landlord and his wife and two or three others, who have stayed behind to help clear up the mess, the rest of the night's audience having already made themselves scarce.

Honesty goes round the drovers inside and out and arranges how they are going to spend the night keeping an eye on the herd and on the inn. As he does so, he can't help but think to himself that this drive is not going at all smoothly and finds himself saying out loud to Rhys, 'What else can possibly go wrong?'

'Do you want an answer to that? If so, I can give you a list, starting with the fact that Idris reckons that we are in for a few days' rain from tomorrow morning, which'll check our progress more than just a little bit.'

Guto walks over to them, with a cheeky look on his face.

'Rhys. I've been wondering if the reason they tried to torch the place was that they heard you were about to sing!'

'Very witty, Guto! For you!'

17

Rhys sits with his back against a stone shelter. He has arranged blankets on the ground and despite feeling cold and tired, he has had a good few restful hours since he took over watch in the early hours of the morning and no problems to deal with.

The dawn is slowly streaking across the sky and he can now make out the looming mass of the nearby hills.

There is a redness to the dawn which shows Idris is going to be right about the weather, he thinks, as he shifts uncomfortably to have a good look around.

It is not long before what little dawning visibility there had been disappears and the blackish skies now start to ooze rain, gently at first, all over him. He stands and gathers up his belongings to take into the shelter and carries on watching the weather worsen very quickly indeed.

As if he has a spiritual link to the weather gods, Idris appears.

'See, like I said, we're in for a shocking storm. We won't be going anywhere quickly this morning and we'll have our work cut out keeping this lot tidy. You might as well go in and get some breakfast down you. It's going to be a long old day.'

The thunder and lightning start as Rhys makes his way back to the inn and he is thankful to be greeted by a roaring fire, freshly stoked, and the smell of warm bread, newly baked.

He sits down with his fellow drovers at the table by the fire, just as Honesty and Guto are debating their plan for the day.

Guto tries to steer the decision his way. 'I think we should head out straight away. There's no need to do the shoeing we planned as the ground will be soft underfoot for the cattle anyway.'

'It'll be murder trying to get over the higher pass today. I say we wait. Get the cattle rested and start again tomorrow.'

'But the rain looks set to continue off and on for a few days. It might get worse.'

'Why are you so keen to get on? The next place we're headed for is a shoddy town anyway, full of people even worse than last night's navvies.'

'Yes, but think how it'll be in a few days time if we delay. It'll be even fuller of the horse fair regulars and they can be a rum lot.'

'It's a Gomorrah town at the best of times, to be perfectly honest, full of dirt and prostitutes. How much worse can it get?'

'Believe me. A whole lot worse, Honesty. I know it better than you as I worked the fairs for a few years and you don't want to believe the half of what I've seen.'

'Alright, Guto, you win. Tell the boys that we'll leave in an hour or so. The shoeing can wait 'til tomorrow.'

Guto goes to tell the men and Honesty stays to settle up with the landlord.

'Tell the magistrate about your nasty experience last night and see what he has to say about it. It'll be better for you if we go, although I doubt that lot will show their faces back here.'

'Cowards they may be, but they're still bullies and we're fearful they'll return when you're gone.'

'Oh, I doubt that. They'll be a couple of counties away by now. If I catch up with them again they'll pay for this, I can tell you.'

18

A few days later

THE DROVE UNDERWAY AGAIN, HONESTY tells Rhys that after their nights of sleeping outside, they are now making for his cousin's farm.

'We'll stay overnight and link up with a small herd he has for me to sell for him. I do the same every so often when he has enough head to make it worthwhile. It'll be good for you to know where he is for future reference.'

'What about this town nearby that even Guto thinks is rough? It must be diabolical in that case.'

'Oh, it's that for sure, although it seems strange that a horse-trading town like that can also be called a one-horse town! Nothing much usually happens and it's dead quiet there except at the same time every year at the horse fair. Then you get fights and all sorts of crime. We'll try and dodge all that.'

'Will any of the men go into the town for the night to see the fair?'

'Well, they're grown men, so yes they're free to do so, but I don't advise it. Guto will go, as he's got friends there, but I doubt any of the others will.'

Intermittently, the rain beats down hard as it has for the past few days and the progress is slow, especially over the higher ground.

Every member of the crew and the travellers silently and soddenly make heavy weather of this stage. Even the animals seem to be the same – almost as if they can't be bothered to make life difficult for their handlers – with hangdog expressions on cattle and dogs alike.

Fortunately, the distance to be covered on this stretch is not great, either as the crow flies, or even as the track meanders, over the moorland.

No break is allowed, even for the men's refreshment, which is taken on the hoof and, as a result, they make relentless, if slow going. The dogs are bedraggled too and have to be shouted at constantly to keep them at it.

It is a forlorn group of animals and men that makes its way eventually into a very wet, dirty and surprisingly untidy farmyard.

Honesty has had Idris shout loudly to warn his cousin of their approach and he is there at the farmhouse door to greet them.

'Usual field, Honesty! And then get everyone in here by the fire,' is his only greeting at this point, as he turns on his heel and goes back inside.

'Friendly chap, your cousin,' Rhys quips, but Honesty ignores him as he leads the herd through the farmyard and out the other side, where an open gate into a large enclosure gives no room for doubt about the destination for the herd.

Honesty orders the men to stable the horses and put the dogs into the rather ramshackle-looking barn. As they all dismount, they're gratified to see that, inside, it's reasonably ship-shape and at least dry – plenty of hay has been provided in the stalls for the ponies and some food has even been put out for the dogs in a low-level trough to one side.

Guto marvels at that.

'Your man has only just put this out too. How did he know we were coming? And today? And now?'

'Geraint's a sheep farmer in the main, cattle being an afterthought, and he spends most of his time up on the moors. He'll have seen us miles off and headed back to the farm. He's pleased to see us, but he won't show it.'

The men follow Honesty in single file from the barn to the farmhouse, pushing each other at the front door to get quickly out of the rain and by the fire.

The smell of wet dog is overpowering and the farmhouse is as chaotic inside as the farmyard is outside. The only tidy area is a room off the hall where, shut in by a stable door, are four or five dogs – all yelping for attention until stilled by a whistle from Geraint in another room.

Each drover and traveller peers in at the dogs as they pass the room and marvels at how prim it seems in contrast to the rest of the house, which is as higgedly untidy as it is piggedly smelling.

'It's clear he cares about animals more than he does about himself,' Rhys remarks. Honesty hears him and turns and whispers to the men.

'It wasn't like this when his wife was alive. The house and the yard were tip-top then. Geraint couldn't care less about his own living quarters but she did, and he has only ever cared for animals. It's little wonder Idris and him get on like a house on fire, don't you, Idris?'

Idris beams and pushes past to see his soulmate whilst the rest try to stop gagging from the smell. With cries of 'Ach y fi', they push and shove their way to the large and utterly cluttered farmhouse kitchen.

'You'll not find much to eat at the moment, but give me a minute and we can get some chickens killed and plucked so long as Idris helps me. And I even picked a basket of winberries from the hillsides earlier that we can round off with.'

The Doctor and the young master are standing to one side, horrified at what they can see and fearful of their overnight accommodation.

Geraint sees their dismay.

'Don't worry, gents, you can have the main bedroom. It's immaculate. Just as my wife left it. You'll be clean and comfortable, that's for sure. Have a heart for this lot, they'll be squashed into the other bedroom or out in the barn.'

'But where do you sleep, sir?' Robert Williams asks innocently, soothing his still-throbbing and burnt hands.

'Don't worry about me, I'll sleep the sleep of the righteous down here in front of the fire, just as I usually do. Normally the dogs would be in here with me, but I've put them into the front parlour for tonight. Can you hear my wife spinning in her grave at me having the gall to do that?'

With watch duties divided up and the herd attended to, Guto announces his intention to go into town, now the rain has stopped, and asks for company to go with him.

'I'd like to see it,' says Rhys.

This is met with a 'No chance' from Honesty, a chuckle from Guto and an 'Alright, I'll come then' from Richard Price, looking at nobody in particular.

'You'll sell no salt there, Richard,' Honesty shouts after them as the two men make their way out of the kitchen door.

Meanwhile, the chickens are already in the large black iron pot, boiling away above the fire, having been hung, drawn and quartered whilst the drovers were checking the herd.

All those remaining at the farmhouse are sitting and relaxing in the warmth and before too long the two special travellers are summoned downstairs for supper.

'How do you boys like your quarters?' Geraint enquires solicitously.

'Famously, sir,' says young Robert Williams.

'What about you, Doctor?'

'Well, as I have already and will no doubt be sleeping God knows where from now on, I'll look on it as good practice.'

That acceptance and contentment sets the tone for the evening. Interrupted only by changes in those watching the herd or checking the horses and dogs, the conversation is light-hearted with Honesty and the rest of the drovers vying to regale each other with stories of the worst places they have stayed.

As the evening wears on, the stories ebb and flow and the candles are beginning to gutter in their own wax, the dogs become active and noisy. Sure enough, they soon hear the arrival in the yard of a couple of horses and Geraint checks the front door, shouting, 'Who goes there? Friend or foe?'

'It's only us, of course,' shouts back Guto. 'We'll be in in a minute to give you boys news of what you've been missing.'

Some of the men have a storm lantern ready and go over to the barn to help Guto and Richard see to their ponies and then on to take over their watch of the herd.

As soon as the returning two and the two relieved watchmen are in the farmhouse, Guto and an unusually smiling Richard are being pressed for news from the fair. Guto takes control of their tale.

'The whole town was wild, full to the brim with all manner of folk. We managed to find a corner in The Nag's Head but no sooner had we sat down than in walks, guess who. None other than our big, bearded, navvy friend. Thank God he didn't seem to recognise us, which was just as well as he had a right choice bunch of rogues with him.

'We drank up quickly, I can tell you, and left in a bit of a hurry, making our way to The Prince of Wales, which was also packed to the gunwales. You couldn't tell whether you were being frisked by pickpockets or over-friendly locals.

'The landlord knows me and says, "Guto, how are you?" and he pulls me close to him and whispers, "I'd get out of here sharpish if I was you. There's a big, bearded brute of a man looking for you, says you wronged him and he wants to give you and Honesty a good hiding".'

'We didn't need telling twice,' piped up Richard. 'I had to pack away the salt real quick and made no sales as a result. We left proper smartish and rode out to see my sister over the hill from here on our way back. She fed us, thankfully, and talked nineteen to the dozen. She even kept asking Guto why he was called Guto!'

'Well, Guto, what's the answer to that then?' asks Geraint, who seems particularly keen to know.

'You've all heard of the legend of Guto Nyth Brân haven't you, who could run faster than a hare and beat a horse over a distance race? Well, before I was born, it seems my parents won a lot of money on his final race from Newport to Bedwas.

'He won it, of course, but his manager, Siân from the Shop, slapped him on the back to congratulate him a bit too enthusiastically at the end of the race. That gave him heart failure and he died on the spot. It didn't stop my parents later, when I came along, celebrating their winnings by calling me Guto in his memory.'

Richard could not resist adding, 'And if you'd seen how fast Guto moved to get out of town, you'd have thought Guto Nyth Brân himself was back from the dead. Thank the Lord they called you Guto, you certainly showed them a clean pair of heels tonight.'

Honesty was uneasy about all this, despite Guto and Richard trying to make light of it.

'Geraint, does anybody know we're here?'

'I doubt it. You arrived late and in the rain after all. Even I didn't know you were coming for sure.'

'What if they pay that landlord friend of yours to tell them if he sees you, Guto? Can you trust him to keep quiet?'

'I'm not sure. Depends if they offer enough, I suppose.'

'Well, that settles it. We'll have to make an early start. With any luck we'll be a way away before they sober up enough. And we'd better pack some iron tomorrow, Guto.'

That stark warning puts a damper on the evening and they all call it a day.

19

AT FIRST LIGHT, EVERYONE IS roused quickly and breakfasted frugally on a slice or two each of 'there's lovely' bara brith, spread liberally with farm butter, and the herd is soon on the move again.

Idris voices his anxiety that the shocing has still not been done, but Honesty tells him not to fuss too much as there will be little hard drove road going today and they can shoe any real problem cattle over the next few days.

'It's country routes for us the next day or so, Idris, whilst we skirt round the towns and villages and make our way across into England. The herd'll be fine in those conditions and if we can avoid trouble for the next few days, we'll do nicely. We can't afford to hang around.'

The day is bright and the sun is quickly up. The crows and the larks are early birds too and their noise can be heard clearly even over the sound of the herd and the other animals on the move.

Rhys hears the beautiful singing of the birds and, looking high up in the sky, can't resist singing a quick few lines from *The Rising of The Lark*.

Hark! Hark! his matin praise
In warblings sweet the lark doth rise
To paradise above.

He stops, fearing he will be mocked, but even Guto asks him to carry on and so he does, before finishing in fine voice:

Sing and let the wide world hear,
Thy melody so sweet and clear,
Waking longing in mankind,
To follow to those heights untrod,
Yet nearer day and nearer God,
Eternal joy to find!

'Very nice, Rhys, and uplifting,' praises Honesty, 'but now you can ride at the rear…'

'Where we can't hear you,' chimes in Guto.

'Keep a sharp eye out for anyone following and watch for any stragglers from the herd – shout for Idris if you need him to rope any troublesome ones. Don't wait mind, you have to be quick about it or we'll have trouble keeping them together.'

Rhys does as he is told and, although trying to keep a good look out all around him, is quickly deep in thought, going through snippets of talks he has had with the other drovers and the experiences he has had so far.

He realises he has totally underestimated Honesty and the others. His admiration for Honesty Jones in particular has transformed his view of the man and his vocation. Even Guto has gone up in his estimation, each of the others too in their own way. And was it his imagination, but hadn't Guto fed off the camaraderie of the team and grown less prickly?

'On people and dealing with them and in numerous practical ways, they are actually my superiors,' Rhys finds he is talking to himself. He realises that his previous view of drovers was patronising in the extreme.

'They know so much and not just about the animals and how to handle them. They know how to deal with people. They even know a lot more than I do about the world and what goes on around them.'

Rhys reflects on the many conversations he has had with his travelling companions.

With Idris, who has never been to school in his life, he has spoken about animals, knots, keeping dry, keeping your bearings and all manner of country lore.

With Honesty, he has learnt how to read people and how the money aspects of droving are changing all the time.

From Robert Williams, who had been to a proper school, he has heard about Henry VIII's empty legacy of ruined monasteries – like Vale Crucis Abbey that they had just passed, and about William Pitt, the Prime Minister, of whom Rhys was blissfully unaware.

Richard had lectured him, at some length, on salt making.

Guto had held forth on the scandal of two women living openly together at Plas Newydd and had relished shocking his listener with a wide-eyed tale of their scandalous relationship.

Doctor Dai had set out in detail the defeated attempts to end the slave trade and intrigued him with the story of the Mutiny on the HMS Bounty and the eventual return, against all the odds, of Captain Bligh.

And from William Williams, he had gained an insight as to why canals were the future and how William hoped to work on them, shoeing the horses that would be involved in towing the barges.

Rhys realises that this is an education in itself, right enough, not just a job of work. 'Every day is a school day,' he mumbles. 'I've learnt so much.'

He is humbled at the realisation that his feelings of superiority are, in fact, totally unfounded in the face of nature itself and of those who learn by doing and by their experiences of living and working.

'Who are you talking to?' Idris asks and jolts Rhys out of his reverie.

'No one, Idris. Actually myself, I suppose.'

'Want to share it?'

'Well, I've come to the conclusion that you all have so much more in the way of knowledge about the real things of life than I do.'

'That's not how we see it. You're the clever one, with all the music, singing and poetry. We couldn't do what you do.'

'Don't want to do it, more like.'

'No, Rhys, that's not right. I can't do what you can.'

'Maybe so, but I envy your skills with the animals, Honesty's all-round abilities and even Guto's worldliness.'

'Yes, but they envy your talents. We have to work with what we've got. That's what my father drummed into me.'

'It's more than that, Idris. I'm so ignorant of the world. No wonder you drovers are so popular wherever you travel. You spread news and bring back stories and objects we have never heard of before. I want to shake off my old self and change.'

'Hold on, Rhys. Keep your head. Don't forget where you come from. One day it might be all you have left to hold on to.'

Honesty rides alongside.

'What on earth are you two talking about? Pay attention. Look over there! You're about to lose two from the herd unless you're quick about it. Do I have to do everything myself?'

PART THREE

20

Quite some days later

'I'LL TELL YOU WHAT, HONESTY, I'm finding it tiring speaking English all the time.'

'We have the advantage, mind. We can speak privately in Welsh, Rhys, you and I, even right in front of people, and they won't have a clue what we are talking about. They can't do the same.'

'How does my English sound to you? I'm getting a few sniggers at my accent.'

'Just swear at them in Welsh if it makes you feel better, but don't let it rile you. Most of the time it's all good-natured. By the way, tonight is going to be difficult for us.

We have to stay close to the town and I will have to leave the farm and go and see about some financial transactions.

'I'd like to take you with me. I would take Guto for protection, but the herd will need him to be armed and on duty. This is a notorious place for rustlers and Idris is not quite himself.'

'I'm glad you said that, as I've been meaning to tell you the same. What's wrong?'

'Nothing to worry about. I thought he'd perk up once we'd done all the shoeing. That didn't change things one little bit. But we're in England, that's all that's wrong. Idris feels he's a fish out of water. His English is poor and he says people treat him as if he was a simpleton.'

'We'd better warn them at the farm tonight to mind how they go with him.'

'Well, at least we've nothing to worry about on that score. The farmer and his wife and daughter who run the place are as Welsh as you and me. Although I haven't seen him for years, your father and I knew him well in the old days.

'He was a drover like us for many years and did well enough out of it to buy the farm a few years ago. He likes to keep in touch with us drovers by extending his hospitality to a few droves – Welsh ones only, of course – but he bought his farm hereabouts so that it could serve North Wales and Mid Wales, the crafty so-and-so.'

'Sounds like we should have fun once we've got the herd settled and been into town.'

'That's for sure. He'll want to make an evening of it for certain, complete with singing and recitation, and his daughter has a fine voice, I've been told, so you'll have some competition, Rhys.'

'Sounds like it will be a home from home for all of us. Just what we need, especially Idris.'

Rhys rides around the herd sharing his excitement at the prospect of a good night ahead and, spreading what he has just heard from Honesty, he manages to cheer Idris up into the bargain.

This section of the drove passes quickly and by late afternoon they arrive at the farm. No sooner had their warning shouts been heard than their host was halfway down his drive to greet them. Clearly anxious to get involved, he takes over the lead in getting the herd into the main field for the night.

Until the herd is settled, only quick hellos are exchanged. Leaving Idris with a couple of dogs to make sure the cattle and the geese are content, the other drovers and the travellers make their way into the farmyard where those riding dismount and then all stand in a large circle around the farmer.

Honesty steps forward.

'This is Thomas Hughes, our landlord for the night. He was once a drover like us, until he decided to give it all up for an easy life…'

'I made a mistake there, Honesty. Farming is just as hard a life.'

'Enough of that. I won't make any more introductions 'til we are all inside and when your wife and daughter can meet everyone.'

'Fair enough, Honesty. Let me show you where you will all sleep.'

'As you see, Thomas, we have two gentlemen travellers with us. They would be delighted to stay in the house, I am sure, and are ready to pay for the privilege.'

'As they wish. I'll have my wife and daughter make up our best room for them just as soon as they are back from town.'

Honesty and the other men go to the attractive stone building indicated by Thomas. They take the travellers' ponies as well as their own and the remaining dogs with them and walk into an immaculate barn, with the ground floor for stabling and a wooden ladder up to a hayloft where they will sleep.

The travellers are taken inside the house and shown to their room.

In a short time, everyone congregates downstairs in the farmhouse kitchen, a very large room with a few deal-top tables, enough chairs to hold double the number now standing and a large, roaring log fire at one end.

'Well, Thomas, this is a fine welcome indeed. It takes a drover to know a drover's needs.'

'This is more like it,' Guto agrees. 'Why can't all our accommodation be this good?'

'Well, I don't know about that… it's all thanks to my wife really.'

With that, the very bustling wife and very pretty daughter burst into the kitchen and this distracts them all.

Seeing the admiring faces of the men, Thomas introduces his wife, Ellen, and daughter, Mair, as the ladies of the house.

'Hello to you all,' Ellen says brightly. 'We'll make sure you have a good stay with us, won't we, Mair? Now, if you'll excuse us, we'll have to get on and prepare some supper for you all. Thomas, you and our guests can make yourselves scarce for a while.'

Honesty speaks up.

'We'll do that. In fact, Rhys here and I are off into town on business so, Thomas, I'll leave you to make sure the men and our travellers are all settled in. Guto, you can sort out the timings of the men doing the night's watches for me if you please.'

All the men leave the kitchen. Thomas tells the travellers they are welcome to go to their room at the top of the stairs and that he would send the womenfolk to make up the beds. He then goes out with the others and seeks out Honesty and Rhys.

'You'll take care in town, won't you? It's a rough place at the best of times, with even rougher justice. Last week they dragged a pickpocket along the main street behind a horse. No more than a child at that.

'Try and look less like drovers for a start. Take the horse and cart the ladies have returned in and don't wear your hats and all of your usual clothes. You'll find some coats in the barn you can use. I'll show you.'

'Thanks, Thomas.'

'But you'd better be back for supper at eight o'clock sharp, otherwise there'll be hell to pay.'

21

HONESTY AND RHYS STOP the cart outside an imposing building next to The Red Lion, which is clearly the town's coaching inn. A brass plate on the door announces S. Windle Esq., Attorney at Law.

'This is it, Rhys. Simon Windle. He's the man we've come to see.'

'A strange name for an attorney. S. Windle. Swindle! Has he a partner called C. Rook by any chance?'

'D'you know what – I've missed that in all the times I have looked at his name. Actually, Simon is as straight as they come. Let's get inside.'

They knock and are admitted right away by a timid clerk who ushers them into a large panelled office stuffed full of books and with a vast desk piled with papers.

A voice emerges from behind the heap, followed by its owner standing to reveal himself as a tall, upright, distinguished, white-haired and red-faced man in very smart attire, making quite a contrast with his visitors.

Both drovers look at their own garments in dismay.

'Ah, Honesty! I'm always pleased to see you. And who's this young man?'

'This is Rhys, Caradog Morgan's son – he's learning the ropes and doing mighty well, ready to take over from me when I finally retire.'

'Well, there's no finer master to be apprenticed to, Rhys – I'll hope to see you again and again. Now, Honesty, what have you got for me?'

'I've the signed contracts from Sir Hugh – sorry about the delay. Inevitable, I know, but he assures me that all is in order.'

Honesty hands over the red-taped contracts and Mr Windle opens and peruses them.

'Well, thankfully, that all seems to be correct. Now for the payment.'

He unlocks the bottom drawer of his desk and hands over a sheaf of paper to Honesty.

'You'd better count these. They are bearer notes in large denominations. There should be twenty of them. Please confirm that and then sign and date this piece of paper to say you have counted and verified them and that you have taken them into your possession.'

Honesty does as required and carefully places the notes into his saddlebags.

'Thank you, Simon. A pleasure doing business with you.'

'The pleasure is all mine, Honesty. Now, let's have a glass of Madeira to celebrate.'

'Well, if we're quick about it.'

Mr Windle goes to the door and asks his clerk to bring in three glasses of Madeira with all haste.

'Tell me, Rhys. How are you taking to the droving game?'

'Very much taken with it, sir. I had my doubts, I must confess, but I like it more and more.'

'You miss your home, I'm sure, but Honesty has made it work for him, is that not so?'

He turns to Honesty, just as the door is opened by the clerk, who is carrying a silver salver with three full glasses on it.

He has a terrified look on his face, although this is not from fear of dropping the tray, it turns out, but because he has a pistol pointing at his head and is closely followed into the room by the pistol owner, a powerfully built man with a livid scar on his chin, dressed completely in black from head to toe like an undertaker. In tow, another armed man, dressed the same way, enters the room.

Against their black hats and scarves, the ferocity of their faces is stark and scary.

'Don't try nothin' and nobody gets hurt. When we're done, we'll leave you gentlemen to enjoy your drinks. You look as if you could do with them.'

'What in hell's name do you want? You can't come into an attorney's office armed like this and threaten us.'

'Not only can we, mister, but we have done, so listen carefully.'

The man holding the gun to the clerk's head signals with it, in sweeping motions, that the clerk and the others should join each other behind the desk. Both men point their weapons at them and the talker resumes.

'Now, we know you have cash here.'

'Why do you think that?'

'Most attorneys do in our experience. So hand it over.'

'I'm afraid to disappoint you men, but there's no cash here.'

The clerk makes the mistake of glancing nervously at his employer.

'Thanks for giving the game away, Mr Clerk. You can take me to the money or you'll be shot.'

The clerk looks terrified and gives a second glance at his employer.

'Go and get the cash box.'

'Be quick about it. If you aren't back on the count of ten, your boss here will be killed. One…'

The clerk is back by the count of seven.

'Take the box!' croaks Mr Windle.

The silent robber takes the box from the clerk and pushes him back against the others.

'Now, you in the middle, what have you got in your saddlebags. Why are you holding them as if they've precious jewels inside?'

'There are only legal papers in his bags.'

'Who asked you, lawyer. They're not *your* bags. They're *his* bags.'

Honesty takes his bags slowly off his shoulder and places them on the desk in front of them.

Mr Windle goes to snatch them up, but the talker's pistol is waved at his head and he stops.

'So, they do contain something worthwhile, eh?'

'Only legal papers, which are of no value to you but have meant a lot of work for us.'

'Hand the papers over then.'

Honesty opens the bags and gives a bundle of papers to the men.

'Don't, Honesty, don't,' shouts Mr Windle, moving to grab the papers back. Suddenly, *bang!* He is shot for his pains and falls to the ground.

'Now, who's next?' menaces the talker who has fired the shot.

Honesty hands over the papers. The men snatch them and back out of the door with their spoils.

When they hear the front door slam, Honesty takes charge and orders the clerk to fetch a doctor and the local constable.

They cradle the attorney and Honesty tears the blood-stained shirt away from the wound to his shoulder and uses the ends of it to staunch the flow.

'Why did you give them the bearer notes, Honesty,' Mr Windle manages to whisper.

'Don't worry about those now, Simon. Just try and hang on until the doctor gets here.'

With that, the attorney slips into unconsciousness and Rhys begins a whispered conversation with Honesty.

'You don't seem bothered, Honesty, at the loss of a great deal of money.'

'I'm not. I actually passed him some useless accounts papers and a few counterfeit bearer notes which I keep for such a time as this. They can't read, those two, in all likelihood. I don't suppose, anyway. But if they try and use the notes, they will be refused. Unless they can con somebody else to buy them.'

'But where are the real notes?'

'Rhys,' he says, lowering his voice still further, 'I'm only telling *you* this: there's a secret compartment in each saddlebag and that's where anything worthwhile is kept.'

'You'll have to tell Mr Windle – he'll feel a lot better about it all with that piece of news. If he recovers, that is.'

'Oh, he'll recover all right. It's just a flesh wound. He's fainted away, mainly at the sight of the blood.'

'You must tell him though, when he comes round.'

'No, I won't. And neither will you. Doesn't it seem odd to you that the men came at the precise time we were here so we could be witnesses to the theft? They could have come anytime to get those notes. Why wait until they'd been signed for by me? Sir Hugh will be interested in this, for sure.'

'What are you saying?'

'I'm saying that Swindle, as you call him, could be living up to his name. We've been set up. I'll tell the constable my suspicions when he comes, but only if he seems to be an honest man. Meanwhile, get me those signed contracts from the desk. I'll have them too for safe keeping whilst we're at it.'

The local doctor rushes in with the clerk, examines the patient, pronounces him to have to a flesh wound only and then revives him with some smelling salts. A relieved clerk – although, in truth, far more anxious about his employment than his employer – smiles in the certainty that death and his imminent loss of office seem to have been averted and goes off again, this time to fetch the constable.

Mr Windle fully comes to and looks strangely at Honesty and Rhys.

The doctor reassures him that he is going to be all right.

'You've had a lucky escape, Mr Windle, and no mistake.'

'Honesty, please come back in the morning.'

'You won't be compos mentis for that, sir, not after I've stitched and bandaged you and laced you up with laudanum.'

'Nor am I able to return in the morning, doctor,' vouches Honesty. 'We'll be away early. I'll see you, Simon, on my return journey.' Honesty pats the lawyer reassuringly and turns to the doctor. 'And now, after all this excitement, I'll wait outside and leave you to patch Mr Windle up. I'll have a word with the constable when he arrives and then be off. Good luck!'

22

ONCE THEY ARE BACK IN the cart and returning to the farm, Honesty turns to Rhys.

'You can't predict what's going to happen next.'

'Are you sure we were being Swindled?'

'Look, Rhys, there's no need to keep using that joke even though it fits perfectly. The truth is, I'm not certain, no, but until we know for sure, then it's best to be careful.'

'What did you tell the constable?'

'Nothing much. Not the truth and that's a fact. I asked him his name first off and when he said Edward Windle, without thinking, it would seem – you can see why he's the constable of the family and not the lawyer – I decided that I'd skip my suspicions about our attorney and just retell the story of the robbery.'

'What did he have to say?'

'He seemed most interested in whether we would recognise the robbers again. I suppose he would, but even so he kept on about it until he was satisfied that we didn't think we could pick them out again. I laid it on thick about the dimness of the candles in the darkened room, the mufflers wrapped around the men's faces, the hats covering their heads… Oh, and us being too frightened to take it all in, of course!'

'But when we came out and you asked me before the constable arrived, I told you I'd know them anywhere. I saw the first man had a scar on his chin and a Roman nose just like my father's. Then you told me to wait in the cart.'

'Well, I'm sorry I did that to you, but it was better to tell him you said it was too dark to get to see them properly and you didn't think to look that closely at them. I said you were a harpist from Wales and not really of this world. That made him smile – you helped really.'

'Thanks very much. So you think the constable is in on it too?'

'Just say that, in my view, they're as thick as thieves and all in it together.'

'Why did you also want the contracts when you've got the money?'

'They're the contracts to sell some land, one for the vendor and one for the purchaser. Sir Hugh can now have the contracts back and tear them up. So he'll have the land *and* he'll have the money.'

'That doesn't sound quite like Honesty to me.'

'I'm as honest as the day is long. But if the day gets shortened unnaturally and the odds are going against me, a little bit of cunning does no harm. I'll let Sir Hugh take the final decision.'

'But *you* could keep the bearer notes for yourself, couldn't you?'

'Yes, but honesty dictates I wouldn't do such a thing. I only meant that, sometimes, honesty is not the best policy with your enemies and even with some friends.'

'Coming from you, even admitting to stretching the truth a bit is quite something. You never cease to amaze me, Honesty. I can't wait to tell them back at the farm.'

'Look, let's keep quiet about this with the others, especially about me carrying bearer notes.'

'But won't Thomas find out about it on his next visit to town?'

'He might find out about the robbery, but that's all. And we'll be long gone by then. I'll talk to him and explain when I next see him.'

'Just act normal tonight and keep all this to yourself.'

23

Honesty and Rhys are throwing off their nasty experience and are launching themselves into the evening at the farm.

To everyone's surprise, their host, Thomas Hughes, takes charge of the post-supper entertainment, usurping Honesty's usual chairing role.

'Now, first up, I want to go around everybody and for you to introduce yourselves and, if you've a mind to, do a little turn – your favourite song, or recitation, or even a dance.'

Groans greet this announcement, but Thomas swats them aside with waves of his hand.

'I'll go first off, to show the way. There's nothing to it! We'll learn more about each other. Like family, that's how I see it. My name is Thomas Hughes, originally from Kidwelly, son of a farm labourer and a dairy maid, thirty years a drover.'

'Your mother was a drover?' Guto shouts.

'No, no. Me. I was. Thirty years a drover and now I'm a farmer for my sins. Lucky for you I can't perform.'

'Poor Mrs Hughes!' Guto again cuts in.

'On the stage, you fool. So now, I will pass you all to my lovely wife… no, not like that… to introduce herself.'

The men gradually discover that Mrs Hughes is a bailiff's daughter from Camarthen, who rescued Thomas and 'turned him into the man you see before you today'. She then proceeds to say nothing about herself, but concentrates on her 'lovely daughter' and how eligible she is, 'except there is none within twenty miles worthy of her'. Mair has to tell her to stop embarrassing them both.

Then, from Mair, they hear that she sometimes has daydreams of leaving the farm, but they don't last long. Whenever she thinks that way, she says she sings *The Miller's Daughter* and asks Rhys if he knows the music for it on the harp. He does and plays it, with her singing, in a beautiful and moving rendition.

I am the miller's daughter,
And when the mill goes round,
I listen to its murmur
As to a warning sound;

Advice it seems to give me,
As would a dear old friend,
And tells me of the dangers
'Gainst which I must contend.

It tells me to be thrifty,
And not to waste a day,
And how the precious moments
Of life soon pass away —
I may not always hear it,
But where my home may be,
The mill's familiar murmur,
Will be a guide to me.

Glasses are replenished at this stage of the proceedings. The performance goes very well and Mair is congratulated by them all. She and Rhys talk in a huddle.

'Mair, that was truly lovely. You've a rare talent and a beautiful voice. You're right to dream.'

'Rhys, that's sweet of you to say, but my father would never allow me to take it any further. He'd never even let me go on stage or sing in public. He hates it if I even go into town! I'm trapped. I know that. But I really don't mind. That sort of life is not for the likes of me anyhow!'

'I'm in the same boat, Mair. All I live for is music, but I can't live by it. Nobody understands that. I'm trapped too, but I mind, I can tell you. I really do. Playing with you singing just now has brought that all back to me.'

Thomas calls the audience to order and invites Idris to the front.

'I'm Idris Evans…Big Idris if you like… I'm more used to talking to animals… And they don't give me no grief, not like what people do. I'm Anglesey-born, like all the boys and that's really where I belongs.'

'Do your animal noises, Iddy,' someone calls out, with shouts of 'Go on', 'Yes, Idris!' and 'Come on!' from the others.

'All right then. Here goes!'

Idris then, to the astonishment of the hosts, gives a virtuoso turn of bird and other animal impressions and rounds off with several different cow noises, all the while explaining what each one means, before sitting down to great applause.

'You've set the performance level very high, Idris,' announces Thomas. 'Let's give a welcome to…'

The party then hear, at great length, from Richard Price and learn a great deal more than they ever needed to know about the importance of salt and the complications of its production. To catcalls, he has to repeatedly say that, no, it isn't a sales pitch, but adds that, naturally, any orders on the night would get preferential rates.

There are quite a few raised eyebrows as he tells them all that his ambition, more than anything in the world, is to open up a salt trail from Wales to London and make his fortune.

With a few tuts, John Griffiths steps up.

'Never mind salt, Richard, you don't know which side your bread is buttered. I'm proud of being a drover and I don't have any dreams of doing anything else. Count your blessings. That's what I do. That seems rare these days. I've had a good life, but I'm not far off calling it a day. When Honesty goes, so will I. We've worked together man and boy and that's been a privilege for me, *to be honest*!'

Laughter greets this, which gives him time to take up a length of rope and, asking Rhys for some harp accompaniment, John shows off his skills with knots and rope handling.

Guto is next up and is ready for it, having strapped on two of his guns.

'My father up and left his home at seventeen. He couldn't face the disgrace of my mother having me when she was only sixteen and out of wedlock. He ran away to sea and my mother struggled all her short life. My grandparents meant the world to me and they never threw my mother or me out.'

Mair asks, 'Did you ever meet your father, Guto?'

'I saw him only the once when he came back. I must have been about ten or eleven. But he quickly disappeared again. He was full of stories about how he was cook for the captain and the crew on a ship that carried slate out of Portmadoc all over the place. He gave me a dagger that once belonged, so he said, to Captain Harri Morgan, the notorious Welsh pirate. The only other thing I remember about my father is that he had the biggest hands I'd ever seen.'

Then Guto shows his own enormous hands and, working them quickly, draws his guns very fast indeed, spinning round and 'shooting' imaginary vermin of indeterminate human, animal, or even parental, variety, before he sits down to loud cheers.

'Perhaps I'd better introduce myself, before anyone gets hurt.'

With those words, the Doctor stands.

'My name is David Davies. Some folk call me Dai and others use different names but, being a doctor, die is the last thing I'll do. I've tried being a veterinary practitioner, but not being like Idris in any shape or form, animals and I didn't really hit it off. Actually, like a midwife who dislikes children, I was the only veterinary I know who hates animals. It was time to try something else.

'I know that my skills are not held in high regard in Anglesey, so I have decided to try my luck with the Royal Navy. I hate war too, so I am going to try to make some kind of difference to human suffering, however best I can.

'I will always remember this experience and I am full of admiration for the way Honesty has led us all. So far, anyway! Let me introduce you to Robert Williams, my travelling companion – a young man already of great character, like his illustrious father. I expect great things of him, *to be honest!*'

Honesty is quickly up on his feet, 'Please tell me I don't say that all the time?'

'Oh, but you do,' the others all chorus.

A reluctant Robert Williams is hauled to his feet by the Doctor to take his turn.

'Thanks, Doctor, for those few kind words. I'm the son of a successful man, it's true, but I've come to view all the men on this journey as that. I've learnt much to admire on the way and I've felt more at home with you than I did at my boarding school.

'I also feel braver about travelling in Europe on my Grand Tour, but this leg of the journey, I'm sure, will stand comparison with the rest of it. I'm keeping a journal and it's already crammed full of stories and adventures. And it isn't over yet!'

This gets a big round of applause and Thomas is enjoying himself so much that he just about remembers to call the next drover to address the party.

'Who's next then?'

'That'll be me, William Williams, farrier and drover. My family has been in the farrier trade for generation after generation. The trouble is, with three brothers, we've to travel far and wide to get enough work. We're used to seeking it out.

'Perhaps I shouldn't say this now, but I want to thank Honesty for giving me the chances that he has, but after this one, I'm off to try and get work on the canals, with all the horses that are involved. I might stay in London if there's an opening for me. Failing that, I'm going to give America a go. It's a young country, and full of opportunity now it's independent is what I've heard.'

Thomas is then reminded by Honesty that Rhys has yet to perform for them and Rhys stands at this introduction of sorts.

'My name is Rhys Morgan, the son of Caradog – from a long line of farmers and drovers, but until now, not of musicians. Actually, before me, the black sheep of the family was my uncle who left the family farm and droving with my father to become a congregational minister.

'Nonconformist he was, in more ways than one, according to my father, and someone who believed that each of us must work out our own salvation. We've heard why that's so this evening, in everything we've all said, so it's true all right.

'A lot of us are travellers, constantly on a journey as we seek our own salvation. It seems right then that I should sing *As the Night is Approaching*.

As the night is approaching, the light fades away,
And faint and more faint glows the sunshine of day;
The winds are all hushed and the ocean serene,
As calm as the lakes in your valleys so green;
So this is the hour to remember my home,
As far from its beauty I wander and roam;
When the scenes I have loved are re-lived in my mind,
With my heart full of longing for those left behind.

Yes, this is the hour when alone and so blue,
The exile looks back on the days that he knew;
Fond memories flood into heart and to mind,
He thinks he may never find loved ones so kind.
In vain that for him sweetest flowers will grow,
In vain blooms for him that soft landscape we know;
The beauty of valleys and mountains so grand
Makes him sigh and long for his own native land.

This marks the end of the concert party. Whilst they're all showing their appreciation for Rhys' moving singing and playing, Honesty stands and thanks their hosts for not only feeding them so royally, but for allowing them to relax and enjoy themselves so thoroughly.

'It would not have been possible, Thomas, if you hadn't so kindly kept your own men from their homes to keep an eye on the herd for us. We must now take over, boys. Let's give a grateful thanks to the wonderful Hughes family.'

'Hip hip,' shouts Robert and the others all applaud their generous and kind-hearted hosts.

Outside, Guto pokes Rhys in the back who turns, startled, to face him.

'What was that for?'

'For Eunice.'

'What do you mean?'

'I saw you sweet talking Mair. Convenient for you, isn't it, you rotten bastard, that you can forget Eunice so quickly.'

'I'm touched that you have Eunice's best interests at heart, Guto, but, actually, me and Mair were talking about music mainly – until she started asking about you.'

'How was that then?'

'You're a fool, Guto, a blind fool. It's you she likes, not me. I even sang your praises – a short song, I'll admit.'

'What was she saying?'

'Oh, she kept going on about your "hypnotic blue eyes" and your "rugged good looks". The poor misguided creature even thinks you have a "sad and soulful side". She's smitten all right, that's for sure.'

'What should I do?'

'Well, I could go and put her straight and tell her you're an idiot, or you can get back in there now and talk to her.'

24

THE HERD, THE DOGS AND THE MEN, rested after their night off, are making good progress. Rhys and Honesty settle into a good pace at the head of the long procession and are discussing yesterday's events.

'What are you going to do about our robber friends, Honesty? When they discover you've tricked them, they'll not be pleased to say the least.'

'I'm not sure what'll happen next. You can be sure in life that it's never what you think will happen that actually does. Let's put it this way. I'm glad we've got Guto and, if you've not noticed, he's wearing his guns all the time now.'

'Have you told him?'

'Not exactly, no. I think he senses it. All I said was that the meeting didn't quite go to plan and we'd better be prepared for trouble.'

'I saw the way he kept looking back at the farm this morning when we left. Does he think we're being followed?'

'Actually, Rhys, I think he kept looking back at Mair. He's been knocked sideways by her, worse than if he'd been clobbered by those brigands who tried to rob us.'

'Can't say I blame him. She's a real find that one.'

'Did you see them talking at the end last night. They seem to get on like a house on fire. Mrs Hughes was nudging Thomas and pointing at them from time to time. Don't tell me you missed all that.'

'I'm afraid I did. And now I'm too busy thinking about getting to London and finishing the drove to worry about what those two are up to.'

'You can't let yourself get preoccupied like that. That's how you miss things happening in the here and now. With people and animals, it's the same. If you get distracted, you can miss good and bad things or early warning signs of trouble.'

'What do you think Guto will do about Mair?'

'Well, after breakfast they seemed to have a good talk and he said to me that he thought he would call in on his way home to see her again. Maybe if they both still feel the same then, something might come of it. God knows what Thomas will think or say or do when that day comes.'

The day goes quickly and they make very good progress, eventually arriving at an inn in a tiny hamlet on the outskirts of a small town, which brings them ever closer to London.

They put the herd into the two large fields, one behind the other, at the rear of the inn that has, out at the front, a sign hanging above its front door in the form of a five-bar gate. Written on it is the name of the inn, The Gate Hangs High, and, in verse below, the words:

This Gate Hangs High and Hinders None
Refresh and Pay and Travel On

As they stable the horses, Rhys asks Honesty what the other large barn is for.

'This is an unpleasant place to stay sometimes, Rhys, because they have the occasional dog-fighting evening here and it looks to me like tonight is a night for it. I'm not sure if it's over or not. It seems quiet to me.'

During the drove, Rhys has heard about cock-fighting, bear-baiting and all manner of animal-related entertainment, usually where betting is involved and the kind of cruelty that those who work with animals find hard to take.

There is only a low-level hubbub from the adjacent barn, but the drovers' dogs are fully alert, agitated and restless.

'Keep our dogs together tonight, Idris. And tie them up. We'll have to watch them and the herd tonight. You and Guto sleep with the horses and dogs and John and William can take first watch over the herd. Luckily, most of the herd are in the far field and some way away from all the likely action.'

He finishes just as the main door of the larger barn opens and three rough-featured, poorly clothed and unshaven men emerge into the evening sunlight. They see the group of drovers coming out of the other barn.

'Well, well. Look what we have here,' the one carrying a large stick says to the other mean-looking men. 'Drovers.' Then, in a louder voice for the benefit of the whole yard, 'This is a bit of a turn up. Where are you from, lads?'

Guto replies. 'We're Welsh drovers.'

'I said where are you from?'

'You can work it out for yourself.'

Guto is needling them, that much is obvious.

'Well, what do you say to letting some Welsh dogs take on the English and see who comes out on top?'

Honesty steps forward and tries to calm things down before it gets out of hand.

'Sorry, gents. Our dogs are working dogs and far too important to us to risk in a cruel fight.'

'Cruel are we? These are animals. Fighting, that's what they do. We aren't the cruel ones. You are. Forcing them to work for you. Unnatural. That's what I call it.'

He is swaggering now, showing off in front of his supporters.

Fortunately, the large jovial landlord strides over from the back door of the inn.

'Now come on, lads! The drovers mustn't be tested. They are regulars here same as you.'

'Yes, but you make more from us, you old moneybags.'

It is at this point that Rhys realises why most of the landlords he has met on the drove are very large and frightening men themselves…

'Talk to me like that again, Jake, and you'll be looking elsewhere for a place to meet.'

'Well, if the Welsh dogs are too scared to fight, what about a bare-knuckle fist fight – your best man against ours?'

At this point Honesty steps forward again, closer to Jake and feeling bolder now the landlord has intervened.

'My men are just as important to me… a put-up fight is ridiculous.'

'Well, lads,' Jake starts to play to the gallery as he turns to see that quite a few men have come out of the barn to see what all the fuss is about. 'Not only are the Welsh thieves…'

'Taffy was a Welshman, Taffy was a thief,' breaks in a heckler.

'…but they are cowards.'

The landlord looks worriedly towards Guto, who has moved his coat back at his waist to reveal his guns, and then towards Jake who is spoiling for a fight.

'Come on, lads – let's all be friends. What about a bit of sport? I'll give a yard of ale to any man who can beat any challenger at arm wrestling. Come on, Welsh or English, or Scottish, or Irish… Jake, you can take on all comers.'

This seems to take the heat out of the exchange and a table and chairs are set up near the back door of the inn.

It finally settles on Jake as the resident winner, having despatched several men of each camp, but before he can claim his ale, Idris walks up.

'Now let's get this straight. If I win, you leave us alone to get on with minding our own business?'

Jake merely shrugs and indicates that Idris take the seat opposite him. Idris sits and the final wrestle begins. Jake suddenly takes Idris by surprise and nearly forces his arm to the table. Then, with superhuman strength, Idris, bit by bit, heaves and strains and pushes Jake's arm back to the vertical and then, dramatically, to the horizontal. Jake winces in pain and anguish when his arm bangs on the table.

Idris stands in triumph and the landlord raises his arm aloft as the winner.

'Now, lads, a worthy winner against great competition. Let's congratulate him and let him have his ale in peace.'

'It doesn't end here.' It's Jake's sideman who shouts this and follows it up with, 'This has got to be settled in a proper fist fight. Arm wrestling is just the start.'

William Williams is tired of all this and, picking up a small stick from the ground, taps the table with it.

'Will you leave us alone if I put up a challenge and win it?'

The landlord is relieved and quietens Jake and his men with, 'Let him speak. Hear him out. It seems reasonable to me. Now, what challenge have you got for them?'

Despite Honesty and the other drovers urging caution, William continues calmly.

'I will go against your biggest, fiercest dog with just this small stick.'

Jake chuckles. The crowd erupt in laughter and make all manner of derisive comments. Jake holds his hand up to silence them.

'Fair enough. A man versus dog contest.'

'More like English dog versus Welsh dog,' shouts a sideman.

William takes a step forward.

'So now you'll get your dog fight.'

Honesty tries again to intervene.

'Don't be a fool, William.'

'Leave the Welsh windbag to eat his words,' Jake is quick to make sure there is no going back on this challenge. 'All right – our nastiest dog against a nasty Welsh dog.'

By now there's a throng of men outside in the open, from the barn and from the inn. In next to no time, they crowd round to form a narrow corridor – at one end stands an evil-looking dog, more wolf than anything else, straining and snarling at the leash held tight by his handler. At the other end stands William, his arms by his side with the short stick in his left hand.

One man, with a bag of money over his shoulder, goes round encouraging and taking bets, and gets lots of takers as the excitement builds.

At last, Jake asks William if he's ready and explains, taking off his muffler, that he will raise it high and when he drops it, the dog will be released.

The dog's owner, equally wolfish, urges the dog on, pointing at William and repeating 'Kill, kill, kill'.

The muffler is raised. The noisy crowd are suddenly hushed. Down comes the muffler and the dog is unleashed, leaping in the air towards William.

The distance between dog and man is no more than twenty-five yards and is covered in a flash.

As soon as the dog leaps from the clutches of its owner, William crouches down and reaches out with his left arm, holding the stick straight ahead, pointing at the dog.

As the dog crashes towards him, snarling, William, timing his movement to perfection, stands and swiftly moves the stick to the left in his outstretched arm. The stick is now at the same height as his own head and the length of his arm away from his body.

The dog leaps, following the sudden movement of the stick, and, with its slavering jaws, lunges and bites at it.

With the dog in the air, and as part of one continuous movement, William turns, kicks up to his left with his right boot, and makes vicious contact with the underside of the dog's body.

The dog yelps and collapses winded to the floor. Before William can do any more, the dog's handler rushes to take his grounded beast by the collar, yelling, 'Don't kick him any more, what have you done to my prize dog?'

There is uproar and the crowd are shouting their verdict on the outcome of the contest and abuse at the loss of their bets.

The landlord, as if sensing there could be trouble, is already at his back door with a group of his regulars armed with sticks.

The drovers gather round William to congratulate him as Jake advances.

'Cheats. Let's get them, lads. You lot and your cattle are finished.'

Before Jake makes any more steps forward, Idris, incensed by the threat to his herd, is up and at him and lifts him bodily, high into the air.

Honesty, now backed by the advancing landlord and his men in support, shouts at his hostile audience.

'We'll be keeping Jake hostage overnight.'

A thrashing Jake is tied up in an instant by John Griffiths, finding more use for his ropes than party tricks, and Guto draws a pistol and points it at Jake's head.

The landlord, flanked by his own guard of burly men armed with their sticks, addresses them all.

'This has got out of hand. I want you all to disperse and go to your homes. The fun is over for tonight. We'll look after Jake until midday tomorrow and release him then if there has been no further trouble in the night. The herd of cattle and these drovers and their animals are not to be harmed or bothered in any way. It's a serious offence if you do and the magistrates will have a field day with you if you don't all calm down and go home.'

Fortunately they all do his bidding and a lot of disconsolate and poorer men beat a slow, steady retreat out of the inn yard.

The only happy man at the end of the evening, making his way into the inn, is the one keeping a very low profile who took all the bets on the dog to win.

PART FOUR

25

Some days later

'I'VE NEVER BEEN SO PLEASED to see the back of anywhere in my life as I was when we left behind the dog-fighting inn,' says Rhys as he shares his morning's thoughts with Honesty. The drove, now well underway, rests for a short time to let the cattle graze and forage at the roadside.

'We were lucky there. The landlord'll have to watch it or he'll lose his reputation. It's long been a "lock and key" establishment where us drovers can leave valuables and cash because of his reputation as being completely trustworthy.'

'So that's why he was on our side.'

'Yes, his place is used by drovers from all over the country. He won't want to lose that trade.'

'Well he'll have to get rid of the dog-fighting crowd then.'

'That's a fact. I told him as much this morning and he agreed readily enough, telling me to make sure that any drovers I meet know that they'll always have a welcome with him.'

'We've piled up quite a few enemies on this trip, Honesty. Will any of them catch up with us?'

'Only a few days left, so I won't risk our luck by saying anything on that score. I'm more worried now about how the cattle are.'

'They look fine to me, a few a bit thin maybe but only a bit.'

'That's exactly the point, Rhys. We have to get as many of them to London in the best possible condition to realise the best price. The grazier will do the main fattening up, but we must make sure they arrive with him in good order. Our Welsh Blacks – or Anglesey runts as the graziers will insist on calling them – are judged solely on appearance. They must be of coal-black colour with white appendages, broad ribs, high and wide hips, deep chests, large dewlaps, flat faces and long horns turning upwards.'

'And not too thin?'

'Exactly. I've been on droves when we've arrived with emaciated cattle that fetch beggar prices and that can ruin a drover. That's why I'm careful not to overdrive the animals, resting them after an exerting day and making sure we shoe any before they become lame. You can't force the pace, otherwise there's too much of a build up of sweat on their skin and they lose their bloom.'

'Why do we take extra time then in avoiding the turnpike roads – you practically run a mile if you so much as see a tollgate?'

'To continue our lesson, Rhys, it's to make sure we make more money in the end, by not spending too much on the way.'

'But if going cross-country means a longer distance, surely that's a daft way to go.'

'It's a balance, and one learnt through experience. You'll get the hang of it.'

'Will I though? I'm not sure, Honesty, I'm really not. The other night rattled me as much as it seems to have wobbled everyone, even Guto. And what's worse, all the tough things that have happened make me wonder whether I'm the man for the job.'

'Rhys, how can you say that? You're still picking up the reins and learning the ropes. That's why you're doing this drove – and a few more, perhaps – with me. You can hire hard men to help you handle the rough stuff. You've a good head for figures, you can think on your feet and you've got plenty of charm. Those qualities make a successful drover as much as the physical side of things.'

And so the final few days of the drove are spent making gentle progress and in lessons from Honesty to Rhys — the 'master and apprentice' as the other drovers refer to them. In the evenings, at various drovers' inns, the books of account are pored over by both of them, as Honesty tries to drum into Rhys the importance of looking after the money side of things, keeping up with the books and understanding not just how to calculate a profit but how best to make one.

26

'WHAT HAPPENS WHEN WE GET TO LONDON?' Rhys is inquisitive with Honesty, although, if he's being honest with himself, he really finds it the best way of passing the time and happens to learn something in the process.

'We have to sell the animals. I find it better to sell them to a middleman and I've a good one in Islington who's a grazier. He'll give me a good price and then he'll fatten them up if needs be and sell them on. He's a good man and will sometimes give me a bonus payment if he can sell them on well. That depends on him not having too much fattening up to do, of course.

I was lucky to find him and we're working on him to join us in a bank I want to set up with David Jones, a friend who, like me, is a drover, but down south, from

Llandovery. I'm talking about a proper bank like the Ship Bank or the Black Sheep Bank. I meet David a few times every year and he and I swap knowledge about all the sharp practices that drovers have to contend with from forestallers and engrossers.'

'Who?'

'Middlemen who buy cheap and hold the cattle knowing the prices are going up, maybe because there's a war on or something. They're forestallers.'

'And what on earth are engrossers when they're at home?'

'They're the ones who buy up small herds and amalgamate them to sell on.'

'God, Honesty, how do you know who to trust?'

'That only comes with experience and a good deal of luck. My grandmother used to say, "It's better to be born lucky than rich". You'll learn that in time.

'But more than anything, Rhys, I hope you can enjoy loyalty and trust in your life. I've had that from so many people, even if I've had my bitter disappointments too. Loyalty and trust can only exist when they work both ways.'

'I can see that in the men who work with you, Honesty, and have done for so long. My father included. You're a hard act to follow, that's for sure. Easier for me to be the next one to sing a song on stage than take over from you.'

'Tomorrow, Rhys, you can ride to the outskirts of the City of London to meet our grazier and see how that's done. For the rest of the day, we must inspect the animals carefully, making notes as we go, and then tomorrow we'll do a full head count. We can do a rough count when we stop for the night.'

They are soon upon a small country inn with the usual adjoining fields, this time with a special dry-stone walled cattle-shoeing enclosure.

Idris holds the head of the herd steady whilst he, Honesty and Rhys take up position by the entrance gate to the inn's field to inspect the cattle and count them on entry. When they are ready, Idris opens the gate and attempts to keep a steady flow of cattle.

Counting is difficult as the herd pick up the pace. It is soon over. Honesty consults his notes.

'Well, we seem to have a healthy herd, Idris. Did you spot anything untoward?'

'We've got a good clean herd, Honesty, with no contagion, thank the Lord.'

'What about those cases of bloat we had?'

'That was cured with trocar and cannula.'

'The lactating cows with mastitis?'

'That problem was dealt with by William's deft use of his sharpest knife.'

'We're lucky, this drove, not to come in contact with any cattle plague. A few years back, remember, one drover lost most of a herd with infectious distemper and the King's Commissioners were mighty vexed with him for travelling onwards.'

Idris points, smiling, at Rhys and Honesty looks over to see him still gamely trying to count the cattle, jabbing his finger towards each of the cows as they pass in haphazard clusters. He shouts over.

'How many have we got, Rhys?'

'Three hundred, three hundred… and ninety… something, I think? They all look the same to me. I've lost count now! I nearly had it right until you asked me how many!'

'Don't worry, Rhys. We'll do the count again tomorrow. You can rest assured that our buyer will make an accurate count for himself, as well as us. Idris, what was your quick count?'

'He can't know, he was talking all the time,' Rhys complains.

'456. We started with four hundred after the Strait, your cousin added twenty-five, Thomas Hughes added forty and we've lost nine – three lost strays and six lame, which we were lucky to sell along the way, thanks to Honesty's friendly butchers.'

'How have I missed all that?'

'It's all written in the account books – my daily log shows all.'

Honesty consults the book.

'Spot on Idris! 456 it is. We only need to do another count if our figure is disputed at the point of sale.'

27

WITH ALL THE HERD AND other animals safely quartered, Honesty and Idris discuss the shoeing that can be done on site.

'We'll stay two or three days, tomorrow being Sunday in any event, and rest ourselves and the cattle. You can organise any shoeing with William. You'd better check we have enough cues and get more from the village blacksmith if needs be.'

'That's fine by me, Honesty – and this is a grand place to do all that.'

Rhys reads the painted words on the brick wall of the inn:

Seasoned Hay, Tasty Pastures, Good Beer, Comfortable Beds

'Yes, this looks like the place for us.'

The landlord greets Honesty like a long-lost brother and off they go to do the business.

Rhys turns to Guto.

'I had no idea that Honesty was as much a finance man as he is a drover. Have you a head for figures?'

'Not like him. And I'm no good at the bookwork. You're quicker at sums than me.'

'Yes, but you're faster on the draw – people wouldn't dare to try and cheat you.'

'Actually, Rhys, I'm thinking that Honesty is a big man to follow. How say you, we think of teaming up.'

'And why the change of heart? I thought you had a low opinion of me. What was it you called me. A "rotten bastard"?'

'This drove has changed me, Rhys, I'll be honest. I'm rough and ready, I know that. And I think with my fists too much. I know that too. But I can see working with someone else can spread the load. There's good men you can trust and a man needs friends to face this world at home and on the road.'

'Oh, this wouldn't have anything to do with Mair, would it?'

'I don't rightly know. Maybe! It's time I took things a bit serious anyhow.'

'Well, Guto, I feel the same way, as it happens. Let's discuss it with Honesty when we next get the chance.'

It is not long before all the men are sitting down to a hearty supper and drinking the good ale in a small private room at the back of the inn.

Honesty calls them to attention.

'Lads, the drove is nearly over. We've had an adventure, that's for sure. In the next few days, we can catch our breath and get the herd ready. I'll ride over in a day or so and see Laycock, our grazier in London, and start talking terms.

'We'll then take the herd to his lairage at Islington and, depending on his view of the herd, which I'm sure will be favourable, to be honest, we should be through in under a week.

'As soon as I'm paid, I'll settle up with you all. The Doctor and our young squire are leaving us in the morning and riding off into London and onwards, so let's raise a toast to them for good fortune in their next endeavours.'

Glasses are raised, the toast mumbled by the now merry band.

Unusually for him, being considered timid and rather shy, young Robert Williams stands and addresses them.

'I'd like to propose a vote of thanks to you all, particularly to Honesty for allowing us to come along. I can see why my father holds him in such high regard. But I'm not sure whether travellers are safer on droves or not, actually, as they seem to attract more than their fair share of attention from all kinds of ne'er-do-wells and riff-raff.

'Still, you have brought us through safe and sound in the end and we are very grateful. I hope one day that Honesty's character and exploits will be written about, maybe by our poet, Rhys. Perhaps he could be Boswell to Honesty's Dr Johnson.

'I am as wary of my onward journey... *TO BE HONEST!* ... as I am of the good Doctor's. I hear from our landlord that France is now even more revolutionary and all manner of little battles and wars are breaking out all over the place. The Doctor will be busy, that's for sure. I have greatly enjoyed his company and hope he can come safely through the dangers and horrors of war.

'Thank you all and may we meet again someday back home in Wales, God willing.'

They all drink heartily to that. And then drink some more. A lot more. The evening ends with a rousing chorus of *Men of Harlech* before the watch is set and, with 'march to glory' still ringing in their ears, the others retire to their comfortable beds.

28

AFTER A FEW DAYS OF having helped tend the herd and shoe the cattle, Guto and Rhys leave Idris and the others for a moment to go and broach with Honesty the prospect of them teaming up.

'I thought you might still be uncertain, Rhys, and worried about letting go of your musical ambitions. I thought you, Guto, were keen to be in charge. Can you two work together as a partnership? It's not exactly a marriage made in heaven.'

'It's because we are opposites that we think it will work. I want to see what is happening with Welsh music in London, so I might stay a few extra days, but I do feel the urge more strongly day by day to go back to Wales. Maybe I can do the droving *and* the music?'

'A jack of all trades and master of none.'

'That's harsh. I know I've a lot to learn, but... what do you think, Guto?'

'Well, we both have a lot to learn. I thought I was ready, but I know there is a great deal more to all this than I realised.'

Honesty nods in agreement.

'Wise words from both of you. Droving is an art and a mystery, that's for sure, and only learnt by doing. If you're both sincere in what you're saying, it could just work. You'd better pay attention to the next part as this could make or break the drove.

'We meet today with Richard Laycock, an old friend of mine. He has many, many acres of fields and some covered sheds, which I can tell you is unusual. Some lairs are little better than wasteland. Richard even stall-feeds the cattle and believes in resting them well before market. Sometimes salesman buy direct from him before the cattle even get to market.'

Honesty, Guto and Rhys set out for Islington to visit the grazier. When they are nearly there, they ride past some very shabby enclosures where fairly emaciated cattle and unhealthy sheep are penned.

'Where are these from?' asks Guto.

'Could be from anywhere, but you can see what I mean about the conditions. The animals have been given short shrift, in my view, and deserve better. They'll fetch poor prices.'

Eventually, better enclosures, some with cover, hove into view and the high quality of the livestock is clear even to Rhys and Guto.

'This is your man's place then?' observes Guto.

'Yes, indeed. And look over there. That's him – the large man with his back to us. Those other men with him, facing us, they'll be salesmen.'

'How on earth do you know that from here?' enquires Rhys.

'Simple. They have ink bottles attached to their waist-coats, ready to take orders.'

This draws laughter from Guto and Rhys as the three men get closer to the group and Richard Laycock turns and sees them. He is clearly delighted to see Honesty and when they reach him he is positively beaming.

After the drovers dismount, introductions are made and handshakes exchanged.

'Perfect timing, Honesty. Well met indeed. I have the Collins brothers with me, Henry and Bill,' Richard says indicating each of them in turn, 'two finer salesmen Smithfield has never seen! Gentlemen, meet Honesty Jones, a prime cut of Welsh drover if ever there was one.'

'Richard, thank you. That's some introduction for us, isn't it? Let's hope we don't disappoint. In turn, let me present to you Rhys Morgan and Guto Jenkins, two young men you will be seeing a lot more of over the coming years as they'll be taking over from me.'

Introductions are completed and pleasantries follow as Richard and Honesty trade more compliments. The Collins brothers make to be off, 'not to intrude any further', but Richard stops them and beckons them back into the group with his outstretched arm.

'If you've time, and would like to beat all the other salesmen to it, let's all ride out now and inspect Honesty's herd on the hoof. What d'you say to that, Honesty?'

'Fine with me! We've over four hundred Welsh Blacks, already in nice condition, a short way off at the usual inn. Now's as good a time as any for us.'

With that settled, the grazier and the salesmen are soon mounted on their own horses, tethered close by, and the six ride off at a leisurely pace.

They have not gone far when, approaching at a gallop, comes William Williams who pulls up when he reaches them.

'Honesty,' he splutters, out of breath. 'Am I glad to see you.'

'Steady, William. What's happened? Take your time.'

'Shortly after you left, four men arrived asking for you. I was upstairs and, hearing the commotion of their arrival, looked out of the open window. They stopped John and Richard just outside saying they had urgent business with you. Then it happened very quickly.

'John must have smelt a rat because he refused to tell them where you were and was struck to the ground. Richard was grabbed as well. The men were armed, so I went to the back of the inn, climbed out onto the roof and made my way to the barn. All the time, I could hear shouts from the inn and a shot was fired. Idris was with the herd, so I just saddled up and rode out as fast as I could. Have I done the right thing?'

'What did they look like? Did one have a nose like Caradog's and a nasty scar on his chin?' asks Rhys.

'I'm not sure. I couldn't see their faces from above, but they were all dressed completely in black.'

Honesty and Rhys look at each other, acknowledging in an instant that they recognise the description, which is obvious to the others.

'Who are they, Honesty?' Richard Laycock asks.

'We think that they're the same men that tried to rob us when we were staying with Thomas Hughes, two of them anyway. We tricked them and handed over worthless pieces of paper. It's complicated. We'd better go. Sorry, but the herd inspection will have to wait.'

'Hang on, Honesty, we can't let you go without us,' replies Richard. 'We'll come, won't we, boys? Make up the numbers. The Collins brothers here look pretty frightening, at least to me.'

'No, it's not your fight, Richard.'

Richard reaches out and restrains Honesty's pony as he turns to the others.

'Honesty stood by me in my early days when I was starting out as a grazier and stood up to the bullying of those who were determined to drive me out of business. It's thanks to you,' he says, turning to Honesty, 'that I even have a business. You could have turned your back on me like the other drovers, but you didn't. I won't turn *my* back on you. You say it's not my fight. It is now.'

Rhys intervenes.

'Look, it's Honesty they're after. Why don't the rest of us go back and leave Honesty some distance away. We can fob them off, perhaps, and tell them he's gone back to Wales or something.'

'That's no good,' Guto adds. 'They've probably made the lads talk by now.'

'Guto's right. And anyway, I can't shirk this. And if we're all to go, at least let's have a proper plan.'

After telling the story of the original attempted robbery and how they had duped the rogues involved, Honesty quickly moves on to talk about the layout of the inn and the barns.

Then, after a check on the weapons that they each have in their possession, the men move off at a steady pace in the direction of the inn, their faces full of resolve.

And fear.

29

As they approach the inn, the group fan out so that the seven of them are spaced several feet apart in a formation that resembles ships of the line readying for a naval battle.

No sooner have they arrived, than the front door of the inn is flung open and the landlord is pushed out. Stumbling, now more red-faced than ever and breathing rapidly, he puffs his way towards Honesty.

'There are four men to see you. I am to act as a go-between. They say you tricked them and they've come to put things right. You are to give me your saddlebags and I am to take them inside. They will then leave and that will be an end to it.'

'Tell them they'll have to come and talk to me, or we can fight it out.'

'You're not serious, Honesty, are you? What on earth is worth more than our lives? They mean business this lot, I can tell you. I've known some nasty pieces of work in my time, but these men really scare me. Just give them what they want.'

Honesty whispers to the innkeeper.

'Don't worry. We have a plan.'

He then says loudly, for the benefit of the men inside, 'Tell them to come out and talk face to face.'

The go-between goes back inside and the door closes. There are raised voices. Then, slowly, the front door to the inn opens and the innkeeper is once again pushed violently out and falls to the floor.

He is followed by three men in their telltale black clothes, holding pistols to the heads of Idris, Richard and John, who has bloodstains on his head and looks in a bad way.

Finally, the leader emerges – the scar on his chin more livid than ever – and kicks the innkeeper, who is now on all fours, back to the ground and points his pistol at Honesty.

'You! Drover Jones! Think you're a clever dick, don't you. This time you'll give us what we're after. Those saddlebags, hand them over, or we'll kill your men, starting with the one who's half dead already.'

'You got what you deserved when you tried to rob us. I'm carrying no money. I've taken it all to a London bank today.'

'Come off it, old man. You don't expect us to believe that, do you? You've been with a grazier today, according to your men and, to look at him, he's the big man next to you. Looks like he's been fattening himself up too. Ready for the slaughter. Perhaps we'll start with him.'

His men laugh at this, glad to be able to relieve some of the tension.

'I can't give you the saddlebags. You can have what's in them. That's all.'

'You can't expect us to fall for that again. We know about the secret compartments.'

Rhys has a sudden realisation, which he voices without thinking.

'You can only know that from old Swindle himself.'

He turns to Honesty.

'Swindle must have overheard us when we thought he was out for the count.'

Swinging his gun and his head round to point and stare at Rhys, the gang leader laughs.

'Old Swindle. I like that. Very funny. But you're right. He just wants back what came from him. So we are within our legal rights. Hand over the bloody bags now. I'm running out of patience.'

'Like I say. I can't give you the bags. My mother made them for me. Even you must have a mother and, just as surely, you must love her. The bags are all I've left to remind me of her. Have a heart.'

'Spare us the sob story. Just hand them over or we'll kill one of your men.'

'Can I just explain to you some simple arithmetic. There are four of you. There are eleven of us. Each pistol has a single shot. You have four pistols, which makes four shots. Ignoring your hostages, we have seven pistols and that makes seven shots. You cannot win.'

'Oh, and we've got this.'

Richard Laycock, taking advantage of all the talking, has discreetly raised a rather large and vulgar rifle from its leather case next to his saddle.

'My trusty blunderbuss.'

He points it straight at the ringleader.

'This would probably take your head clean off.'

The weapon is truly frightening, but doesn't quite have the desired effect.

'Listen, grazier. It's probably not even loaded.'

'Are you willing to take the chance?'

'In a word, yes. We'll start by finishing off one of the old drovers. Kill him, Foxy.'

'Don't be a fool, Charlie,' shouts the ginger-haired man holding John Griffiths.

Momentarily distracted, Charlie, the leader, turns his attention to Foxy who has, by now, taken his pistol away from John Griffiths's head. John, summoning up his remaining strength, hits out at the pistol which Foxy, in the struggle, discharges into the eaves of the inn.

At the same time, Idris and Richard turn on their own captors and try to overpower them, but Charlie jumps aside and turns his weapon on Honesty.

A huge bang, as the blunderbuss is discharged, blows Charlie's hat off and throws him off balance, so that his pistol is discharged into the air.

Quick as a flash, Guto is off his horse, with one of his pistols out, and is racing up to Charlie who is sitting on his backside next to the innkeeper.

Guto has the presence of mind to cock his pistol and hold it next to Charlie's head.

'One move and you're dead.'

Honesty, still on his pony, moves forward.

'Charlie. We'll be keeping your weapons. You can ride back to old Swindle and tell him he'd better get out of town fast —and that goes for his brother the constable too. I'll make sure they never work there again. The same goes for you and your gang.'

Guto and the other drovers make sure the gang hand over all their weapons and leave the inn. Honesty, meanwhile, tends to John Griffiths's head wound. It turns out to be superficial, even if the blow has made him feel dreadfully groggy and muzzy.

The innkeeper is quickly recovered from his ordeal and offers brandy all round.

'The blunderbuss saved the day, Richard, but how did you manage to miss him?' asks Honesty.

'Well, for a start, I've never fired it before. For another, he was right; I didn't even know it was loaded. It was my father's and I only keep it for show. You know, to frighten off people.'

'You certainly did that all right!'

The Collins brothers both talk excitedly about the ordeal.

'Well that beats a day selling cattle!'

'I liked the way that firing the blunderbuss nearly knocked Richard clean out of his saddle.'

'And that's saying something, with him fattened ready for slaughter, as the man Charlie said.'

'Enough laughter at my expense,' chides Richard good-naturedly. 'Let's get on with doing what we came for and take a look at Honesty's herd.'

While they do that, Rhys asks Honesty why he lets rogues and villains go scot-free.

'That's easy to answer, Rhys. We are drovers. We have to keep moving. The cattle drive us. We can't waste time getting caught up in the law. Rough justice I know, but we keep moving.'

30

A few days later — Sunday

'Tomorrow, we'll all be up early to take part of the herd now in Islington for the final drove to Smithfield. Laycock's men will take the remainder of the herd as and when.'

Honesty is talking to the men over a hearty breakfast of bacon and eggs.

'Today is a day of rest for us all, apart from Idris, maybe, who'll stay with the herd no doubt. I'm going to take myself off to the Welsh chapel. Who'll go with me? Anyone else interested?'

There are no immediate takers, so Honesty tries another tack.

'Rhys. You need to sing every day, don't you? Well here's your chance.'

'You've already told us that we'll all be up at one o'clock tomorrow morning, can't we just sit around here today? I can sing to myself or for the others right here happily enough.'

'Take him with you, for God's sake,' pipes up Guto, 'we could do with a quiet day ourselves.'

'Yes, you're coming with me, Rhys, and that's an order. I want to show you the chapel and show off your singing skills to the congregation – most are Welsh exiles. They'll want to hear stories from home and they love to meet kindred spirits.'

Honesty and Rhys are soon on their way.

'So, where is this Welsh chapel we're going to?'

'It's in Wilderness Row in Clerkenwell.'

'Wilderness Row – is that symbolic of something?'

'I doubt that, but I agree it's a good place for it. To be honest, Rhys, I wanted you to come with me for company and so we could have a word. Nothing serious, mind, just chewing the cud.'

'I know you by now, Honesty. Something's on your mind. What is it?'

'You haven't mentioned Eunice recently for a start.'

'Oh, haven't I? Nothing odd in that is there?'

'Well, you must be keen to get back to her. Or aren't you?'

'Yes and no.'

'How so?'

'I'm just wondering if I'm ready for all that. I still want to take myself further with the music. Now we are closer to London, maybe I should see more of what is happening there. The innkeeper is a jolly soul and he has been telling me how popular Welsh songs are on the London stage. It's just set me thinking that's all.'

'Are you sure that's all? It's just that you're a young man, like I was once, and you should really be aching to get home to your girl. Are you sure there isn't more to this? After all, absence is supposed to sweeten a fond friendship.'

'No, no. Eunice is still the one. It's just my life in Wales maybe can't compare.'

'I thought you and Guto had settled on taking over. If you've still doubts, you ought to share them with us, Guto included. And Eunice come to that.'

'Yes, I know I should. But I really don't know.'

'Well you'd better decide soon. Our work is very nearly done.'

'Actually, Honesty, there's a favour I want to ask. And it could help me make my mind up once and for all.'

'What is it? Ask away.'

'I heard you and Richard Laycock discuss that the herd would probably be sold in two main lots – some tomorrow and then maybe some in a week or two. He said something, didn't he, about the price moving upwards and upwards as the wars against France take hold. You said that he pays you an extra commission if and when that happens.

'How about I stay around for a week or so to collect the money and see what's what in London?'

'Really?'

'Yes, I'm perfectly serious. It'll give me a chance to perhaps get it out of my system once and for all.'

'Or not, as the case may be?'

'Yes, I suppose that is also a possibility.'

'Well, all right, Rhys. But I don't like the sound of it. You're taking a real risk here and you could lose a lot more than you think.'

'Thanks, Honesty. I can't thank you enough.'

'I just hope, for your sake, that we're doing the right thing letting you stay on. I myself will go off to see my brother down in Kent for a week and will call back through London to see you. Hopefully, you'll be ready to accompany me back to Wales.'

'I didn't know you had a brother.'

'Yes, I've three in fact. This one's in Kent working for a grazier we used to use many years back. He couldn't stand the drover's life and wanted to settle down so he took a job down there. In England! Who'd have thought it?'

31

RHYS AND HONESTY ARRIVE AT THE CHAPEL, a very nondescript building, never mind nonconformist. Rhys knows from Honesty that it's a Welsh Presbyterian chapel that started life in Cock Lane, Smithfield.

As they tether their ponies outside, Honesty is greeted, seemingly, by an old friend.

'Honesty. How nice to see you again. It's a year or two since you worshipped with us.'

'It is that. I've brought along one of my young drovers, Rhys Morgan, who fancies himself as a bit of a poet and musician.'

'I guessed that from the harp, Honesty.'

'Well, any chance he could sing today?'

Rhys looks uncomfortable at this direct approach.

'Don't feel obliged, Mr…'

'Wallis… and it's no trouble, Mr Morgan. In fact it'll be a good day for music, and for Wales, as we have Edward Jones here as a special guest today.'

'What, *the* Edward Jones?'

'Yes.'

'*The* Edward Jones, the harpist, the man who published *Musical and Poetical Relicks of the Welsh Bards*?'

'Yes.'

'The Harp-Master to the Prince of Wales?'

'Yes, yes. The very same.'

'I can't believe the luck of being here on the same day. Honesty, this is almost too good to be true.'

'Pastor Wallis. This'll either be a very good thing for my friend Rhys, or a very bad thing. His life may turn on it.'

'Well, let's go in and try and make it a good thing.'

They enter through the double doors and the small, simply furnished, wood-panelled chapel is already full, as Rhys and Honesty sit down at the end of a pew, at the back, where space is readily made for them.

It's as if in a dream that the service takes place, for Rhys is thinking of what he might play and what might follow on from the chance meeting with Edward Jones.

Pastor Wallis keeps the formalities short and introduces Edward Jones.

'Our guest today is well known to you all, and to all of Wales it would seem. He's from a musical family and follows in his father's footsteps. Teacher, arranger and publisher of harp music, he's now harpist to the Prince of Wales.

'The only thing he can't do, apparently, which his father could, is make harps. But he can certainly make them sing, as he'll now demonstrate.'

The recital is wonderful and the appreciative congregation are wildly enthusiastic about the singing and playing they are so privileged to be listening to.

Rhys is incredibly impressed and completely in awe, suffering a real crisis of confidence in his own abilities.

During the final applause, Pastor Wallis talks to Edward and when, eventually, the clapping subsides, he waves his hands downwards to call for calm and silence.

'Thank you... I have just spoken to our honourable guest and he has agreed to allow a young drover, just arrived from Wales, to step forward and play with him. Please welcome Rhys Morgan...'

Rhys reluctantly makes his way to the front and, when he arrives and is introduced to his hero, protests that he is not good enough to share the same platform. They have a hushed conversation all the same.

His protestations are brushed aside by Edward Jones who announces to the expectant audience, 'Rhys Morgan is even more reserved than I am and believe me when I tell you, that is really saying something! However, he is, I can tell, a young Welshman, just as I once was, and he is, I know already from our brief conversation, entirely comfortable with our great bardic tradition. He and I will try and recreate an eisteddfod atmosphere today by having a duel in the style of penillion, where we will improvise verses sung to the accompaniment of the harp.'

What follows astounds the audience and, indeed, each of the performers, who are raised to greater and greater heights of singing and playing by their competing individual virtuosity. Edward reluctantly brings the extended penillion to a close to huge acclaim.

Pastor Wallis joins the entire congregation, on their feet, showing their appreciation for the rare display of consummate musicianship.

'Fellow worshippers, we have today witnessed, in the sight of God, a truly magnificent celebration of Welsh music. When Iolo Morganwg formed the Gorsedd community of Welsh bards in June 1792 at a ceremony on Primrose Hill, this is the music he would have given his eyeteeth to hear performed on that occasion.

'Thank you, both of you, but especially Edward for graciously allowing a young upstart to share the stage with you today.'

As the congregation disperses, Honesty makes his way over to join Rhys, Edward and Pastor Wallis, who is busy congratulating Rhys on his abilities. It is with a heavy heart that Honesty speaks.

'Rhys, my boy. Well done. And very well done to you, Mr Jones. You will have turned the boy's head, that's for sure.'

'He's a great talent. I was just telling him that when I first came to London in 1775, I was taken up by a rich patron, Charles Burney, who secured me many pupils for my harp teaching. As a matter of fact, I was approached only the other day by a wealthy gentleman by the name of Sir Charlton Musgrove, who is seeking a Welsh harpist to help him arrange a series of concerts at Drury Lane. I think Rhys here could be the man to do it. And what a start to life in London that would give him.'

Rhys looks uneasily at Honesty who replies, 'Well, Rhys is still, officially at least, a drover. For how much longer, I don't know.'

'This man was born to play music. It has to come out. Look, at least let me arrange a meeting with Sir Charlton. What's the harm in that, I ask you?'

Rhys provides Edward with the name of their inn and after many mutual exchanges of flattery and thanks, Edward says he will send word to the inn if he manages to secure the meeting.

As they leave, Honesty sighs.

'Well, Rhys. What have I done? I've put temptation in your way and, after that performance, even I'm not sure what your next move should be.'

'I think you have shown me the Promised Land.'

'No, don't say that, Rhys. Not on a Sunday. There is no such thing as Heaven on Earth. Remember that. If you think there is, I can assure you it's an illusion — to tempt you. And can I say this: I'm not sure that Edward Jones, for all his success, is actually a happy man. Can you say any different?'

'I think that's *your* reading of him, Honesty, not mine. What I would give to be in his shoes.'

'Think carefully, Rhys. It could be that you give too much.'

'I'm not going to be selling my soul. Honesty, you're too suspicious by half.'

'Am I? If this Sir Charlton Musgrove is such a good catch, why isn't Edward keeping him to himself?'

'Probably because with the Prince of Wales as his patron, he doesn't need, or can't have, access to anyone else.'

'You're probably right. I fear the worst though. For you and, to be honest, for me, your father and Eunice. Even for Guto! You'll have your head turned and will you be able to stay true to your values and to who you are.'

'Who am I, Honesty? A drover? A musician?'

'Who indeed, Rhys.'

32

MONDAY MORNING, MIDDLE-OF-THE-NIGHT EARLY, the drovers set off for Islington. They arrive after a short, largely silent journey by the light of the moon to find commotion and great activity, despite the ungodly hour.

Men are milling around – some on horseback, others on foot. In the different lairs of their grazier, Laycock's, the Welsh herd is being organised.

The drove to Smithfield is a frightening affair conducted by torchlight, with men shouting and dogs barking.

Through the narrow streets, with the constant risk of strays being lost down dark alleys, Honesty and his men guide the part of their herd that is to be sold on straightaway through the maze of streets, glad to be led by Richard Laycock himself, his large bulk astride his sturdy horse, holding aloft a large and blazing torch that, bigger even than his blunderbuss, acts as a beacon to the drovers.

The tortuous final drove is far worse than anything encountered so far. In distance, it is nothing. In difficulty, like nothing else they have experienced so far.

The tumult of cattle and men arriving from all directions is so overwhelming that Idris is almost driven to panic and they are more than a little bit lucky not to lose cattle on the way.

Arriving at Smithfield, they are amazed to pass over ground that is thick with mud and cattle filth – worse than any farmyard, field, moor or bog they have ever encountered.

The animals are fretful and steam rises from their sweaty hides. In certain areas, slaughtering is already taking place, with animals being poleaxed and butchered in the open, their blood mingling with the already smelly and squalid mire to create a fetid mixture underfoot.

The noise of the cattle screaming at their death is horrendous and Idris is sick with the horror of it.

They are so glad to finally reach the penned areas where their animals are to be held. Only a hundred head have been brought to market, as Richard Laycock and the Collins brothers have decided prices are going to be much higher over the coming weeks.

Honesty has agreed to it, needing only the proceeds of a partial sale to enable him to settle up with the men at this stage.

The day at Smithfield is an assault on the senses and by lunchtime, when all the trading has been done with their herds, the grazier, the salesmen and the drovers repair as previously arranged to the Fortune of War, a hostelry at Pie Corner, the junction of Cock Lane and Giltspur Street. Careful directions have been given to each of the men by Richard in case they were to get separated in the crush of men and animals. This is Honesty's local when he's at Smithfield, despite its rather dubious reputation.

When they arrive, the landlord tells them that a certain Sir Charlton Musgrove is waiting for them, or more particularly for Mr Rhys Morgan. Rhys explains that he has left word with their own innkeeper as to his likely whereabouts, in the hope that Edward Jones would be true to his word and make an introduction for him.

Their eyes follow the direction in which the landlord points and there, by the far wall, sits a very obvious and ostentatious bunch of theatricals.

'They'll be your new friends, Rhys,' Guto says shaking his head.

'Go and introduce yourself, Rhys, but then, if you don't mind, please come back and join us. I want to say some thanks and farewells.'

'Of course, Honesty. I'll not let them spoil our final day.'

Rhys spends some time huddled in conversation and, after much ribaldry and backslapping, returns to the corner where the cattlemen are seated.

'Well, Rhys,' asks Guto, 'are you with us or with them now?'

'Steady on, Guto. Let him speak,' Honesty gestures to Rhys to pull up a chair.

'What's all this? Dissension in the camp?' Richard Laycock picks up on the air of uncertainty that has taken hold of the table around him.

'It's just that there may be an opportunity to play some music in London before I return home to Wales.'

'*If* he returns to Wales, more like,' Guto cannot resist adding.

'Nothing has happened yet. Edward Jones – harpist to the Prince of Wales,' Rhys explains to the table, 'has made an introduction for me, that's all. I'm to meet with Sir Charlton Musgrove, the older man in that group over there, and the man who owns the theatre in Drury Lane. Sir Charlton wants to put on an evening to celebrate the music not just of Wales but of all the British Isles, in a show of patriotism.'

'Ah, European wars again. Driving up meat prices and now theatre tickets.' Richard Laycock is evidently bored with the conversation straying too far from the commerce that drives his world. 'Honesty, I'll be away now. Come back with us to Islington where we can settle up for now.'

'Right away, Richard. I'll do that and I'll meet with the rest of you back at the inn later. We can then do our own settling up there. Guto, you can come with me. As I'll be carrying money, you'd better be my bodyguard. Rhys, you'd better go back with the others.'

Guto and Rhys exchange puzzled looks and Rhys shrugs, acknowledging the slight.

33

WHEN RHYS AND THE MEN return to the inn, Guto and Honesty are already there, Guto sitting with the innkeeper.

'What kept you?' asks Guto. 'We have been back for a long time. Honesty's upstairs scratching away at his accounts, trying to make a final tally.'

'Well, this lot kept stopping at various hostelries, buying me drinks and telling me not to be a fool and throw my life away. It was as if they were acting on instructions from Honesty.'

'Now you're here, I'll tell Honesty and we can have our last repast together. Tonight won't be wild and raucous as, apart from Rhys, we all have long journeys ahead.'

John, William and Richard go out to find Idris, the innkeeper goes to start rustling up victuals for the evening and Rhys sinks into a seat next to Guto.

'Where are you off to tomorrow, Guto?'

'You know that already. I can't wait to be with Mair again. I can't understand why you aren't in a rush to be with Eunice. And come to that, what'll I tell her when I get back without you?'

'She'll understand. She knows I have to give this my best shot.'

'Rhys, I hope you know what you're doing. Honesty is worried.'

'I know that. He couldn't even face having to speak to me when we left Smithfield.'

'You should hear him talk about you. "For an intelligent man," he says, "Rhys makes a very good fool." Yes, it's got a lot to do with him fretting about who'll take over from him, but he cares about you, Rhys, and feels responsible to your father. He's already worried about how Caradog will react when you don't return. He's determined to get you to go back with him when he comes back through London from seeing his brother in Kent.'

'Well, I'm not sure about that. I won't have done the theatre by then. He knows that. I'm to come back once we have the rest of the money from Laycock.'

'So at this rate, the dogs will get back first, having made their own way home, once we've let them go in the morning. Then it'll be me, even stopping a day or so with Mair, because I am keeping my pony. With William off to jump into the canal business, it will then be Idris, Richard and John walking back to Wales. Maybe Honesty will arrive at the same time as they do. It'll be maybe a month before you return. That's a long old time. No wonder people are worried you might not actually be coming back.'

'We'll see, Guto. We'll see.'

34

THE MORNING FAREWELLS ARE TINGED with sadness, much as the night before had been.

With accounts drawn up, the men paid and departed, Honesty and Rhys are the only two remaining.

'Well, Rhys, this is it. I'll be off, but back in a few days or so. If you're not staying here, please leave word of where you are so that I can come and find you.'

'Yes, sure. You'll need to let me know about Laycock's timing for the balance of the funds. I'll pick it all up for you.'

'And bring it back as soon as you have it.'

'Of course, of course.'

'You'll have to be careful. Cash or bills of exchange will make you a target. Don't tell anyone you're a drover or they might get ideas that you're carrying something worth stealing.'

'Don't worry, I won't be telling anyone I'm a drover! I'm a musician for the next week or so.'

'Not ashamed, Rhys, are you, of being a drover?'

'No, no, no. Not at all. I didn't mean it like that. I…'

'Never mind that now. Rhys, don't be swayed by glimpses of this life down here. It's what's turned many drovers' heads. Keep yours. Watch out for these new friends of yours. I've tried to show you how to negotiate, but one more rule to follow is always negotiate, then drink, and not the other way round. Insist on a contract for anything you do and read it properly before signing it. Should I be worried that you're innocent of city ways?'

'Honesty, I won't let you down. Honestly!'

'All right then, Rhys. Until we meet again.'

The two men shake hands formally and Rhys goes back upstairs, leaving Honesty to settle up with the innkeeper.

In his room, he sees Honesty riding off and, feeling like a young child again, Rhys finds himself lying on his bed sobbing.

After a while, he gives himself a good talking to: 'Pull yourself together, you've always felt like this at first. You can do it.'

This brings him round and he thinks about making a move to get to his meeting at the theatre later. But he sees the image of his father and Eunice on the far shore on the day the drove started and sobs all the more.

Eventually, Rhys heads downstairs and is pleased to see the smiling face of the host.

'Ah, Rhys. I'm to take good care of you, apparently, and not let you get yourself into trouble.'

'Not much fear of that, kind sir. I'm off to meet a very well-connected man, Sir Charlton Musgrove.'

'Where'll you be meeting him?'

'At the theatre in Drury Lane and then a place called the Bedford Coffeehouse.'

'Stop right there. You have said three or four things that strike terror to my soul. Drury Lane, theatre, Bedford and coffeehouse – all are dens of vice, full of people of easy virtue and loose morals as well as poor food and adulterated liquor. Honesty was right to warn me to look out for you.'

'I'm glad Honesty told me that you were also a lay preacher in the Wesleyan mould. That sounded like a sermon to me.'

'It's easy for you to scoff, but I'm serious. Keep your wits about you and your purse even closer at all times. Watch out for pickpockets. Don't get waylaid and don't let anyone take advantage of you.'

'I understand. I'll be really careful.'

'Good. As it happens, my brother keeps a public house, The Magpie, next to the Fortune of War where you went after the market. Go there if it gets late and tell him I sent you. At least he'll give you a bed for the night so you're not out alone in London.'

They shake hands and Rhys goes off full of a heady mix of hope and trepidation.

35

HAVING FIRST TAKEN A SEAT in the coach that had called at the inn, Rhys, on arrival in the centre of London, is dropped at The White Horse Cellar, a bustling coaching inn on the corner of Albemarle Street. He then carefully follows the innkeeper's verbal instructions, asking the way only a couple of times. Before he knows it, and not quite believing his eyes, he is standing in front of the Theatre Royal.

His sense of wonder soon gives way to apprehension when he enquires inside after Sir Charlton Musgrove, only to be told that he isn't there, hasn't been there and isn't expected. He turns to go and wait outside when his name is called and he sees Edward Jones scuttling down the main stairway.

'Rhys, sorry! Nearly missed you then. The others are round at Bedford's, scheming schemes and planning your future on the stage. Come on, I'll take you there. It's not far, over towards Covent Garden.'

'Why are they at a coffeehouse?'

'You'll learn. This particular place is where a lot of theatricals go, especially on opening nights – it's where playwrights go to find out what people think of their plays. Keep your eyes and ears open, Rhys, you've a lot to learn. And quickly.'

'Will you be taking part, Edward?'

' 'Fraid I can't, Rhys, but I've a few ideas to throw in.'

Jostling their way through the throng, they barely keep within sight of each other and, in a short time, Edward stops suddenly and pulls Rhys in through a door and into the crowded coffeehouse.

'This place has been described as the "emporium of wit, the seat of criticism and the standard of taste", but I find it a trifle annoying. Everyone tries to outdo everybody else with wit and badinage. You'll see. Just try to keep up, or just keep out of it and let the erudite exchanges go on around you.'

They push their way through a series of dingy, wainscoted rooms which are shabbily elegant, the walls covered with gilt frames containing strange curiosities, the whole place stinking of tobacco.

With the loud and animated conversations ringing in their ears, Edward leads Rhys towards a noisy bunch of extravagantly and finely dressed men lounging in a corner with dishes of coffee in front of them; most are puffing on long clay pipes.

Sir Charlton is sitting at the end nearest them and stands when he sees the new arrivals.

'Ah, Edward. How goes the Prince? Are you still plucking for him?'

'No, Sir Charlton, he does that for himself. I merely play my harp.'

'So he does the plucking and you play the harpy?'

Loud laughter saves the need for any further wordplay from Edward, who turns to Rhys.

'See what I mean? And that's just to say hello.'

Sir Charlton addresses Rhys, 'Just a little playfulness. Just ignore him. He can be a little prim, can't you, Edward?'

'I find it all a bit tedious, if I'm honest. We are more direct aren't we, Rhys.'

The other men grow bored at the turn of the conversation and talk amongst themselves and, in particular, to a fleshy-faced man wearing a green frock coat who takes over the lead and starts holding court.

It is quickly revealed that Edward does not really want to take any further part in the theatrical extravaganza planned at Drury Lane. Rhys learns that the green frock coat is worn by the theatre's manager and Sir Charlton has agreed with him to mount an evening's entertainment of Welsh and patriotic ballads and music. Rhys is worried that Edward is not participating.

'But surely, Edward, you will take part. I can't carry a show on my own.'

Sir Charlton guffaws at this.

'No, no, you aren't the star of the show. We want you to do some solo performances, of course, but we'll be using a lot of the ballads Edward has found. You'll also be playing the harp for the other singers, as Edward says you are a fine musician. How does that sound? Not too onerous? Maybe two or three ballads from you and the rest of the time playing the harpy, eh?'

Rhys and Edward exchange looks and Edward takes Rhys by the arm.

'Look, it's time for me to go. Sir Charlton, he's all yours. Rhys, I'll look in at the theatre and find you there in the next few days I hope.'

After Edward leaves, Sir Charlton introduces Rhys to Richard Sheridan, the owner of the theatre, whilst the others look on.

'It's a wonderful theatre, Mr Sheridan.'

'Oh, have you performed there?'

'No, I was there just now in the foyer.'

Laughter greets this reply and Rhys hears a mocking of his accent and a whispered 'A young Welsh lamb to the slaughter'. Mr Sheridan tries to silence the gaiety with his hand, as if calming down a theatre audience.

'Well then, you haven't seen the theatre at all. Wait until you see the auditorium. Magnificent. It certainly cost me enough. I'm hoping these shows of yours will bring in much-needed revenue. Sir Charlton tells me you're quite a talent and you must know that the public can't seem to get enough of the Welsh these days.'

'I've a few ideas of my own and I'm sure that Edward has given Sir Charlton plenty of his, so I'm excited by the prospect.'

'I suggest you go off with Sir Charlton and put a show together. Come over to the theatre tomorrow and we'll finalise the arrangements. How does that sound, Sir Charlton?'

'Perfect, Richard. We'll see you at eleven o'clock and then perhaps we can repair here to celebrate.'

'Capital. You two have a lot to talk about then. You'd better give Rhys a libation or two. He looks like he needs loosening up to get his creative juices flowing.'

With that, he returns to being the centre of attention of his very relaxed group of wits.

36

RHYS AND SIR CHARLTON, with some effort, eventually find a table to themselves and after eating and drinking over the course of a few hours, find they have devised an entertainment which they feel will fit the bill.

Hour by hour, Rhys feels more and more euphoric about how his life is now taking the kind of turn that he only ever dreamt of and never thought possible. Could it be that everything so far has been in preparation for here and now, sitting here, planning a London show?

Rhys has not been judicious in the quantity of food or drink that he's taken on board and, feeling rather nauseous, decides it's time for him to leave.

'I'm afraid I'll have to be on my way, Sir Charlton.'

'The night is young and so are you, Rhys. We've only just started. You can't let the gentlemen of Bedford's think that you're a lightweight. And, in any event, I have a little contract here for you to sign.'

'It looks like a long old contract. Do I have to read it all?'

'No need for that! It's all standard. Edward signed up straight away when he appeared for me. And look, he's doing all right, isn't he? It's exactly what you want to happen, Rhys, certainly judging by the way you've been talking to me.'

'Well it's everything I want and more. What do I do?'

'Look, just sign here. I'll do the rest. Witness your signature. That sort of thing.'

'What am I signing?'

'Just a contract saying that you agree to appear at Drury Lane for a series of dates, with a share of the proceeds going your way. That's all. Look sign here. Use this. I'll dip it in the ink for you.'

As if by magic, Sir Charlton produces the contract, a pen and a bottle of ink and places them on the table in front of Rhys.

Rhys, feeling that he must get outside immediately, signs and, with a barely audible 'See you tomorrow', leaves Sir Charlton's table and makes his way, very gingerly and unsteadily, to the front door and to the outside.

Later, lying in his bed at The Magpie and drifting in and out of shallow sleep, he cannot exactly recall how he made his way from Covent Garden to Smithfield.

He shudders as he suddenly remembers signing a piece of paper thrust at him by Sir Charlton and wonders if he has been a complete fool.

His head aches, he feels incredibly hot and his mouth is as dry as sun-bleached and beached driftwood.

He wakes surprisingly early, especially given the lateness of his getting to bed, the quantity of food he has eaten and the amount of drink he has imbibed since yesterday.

The landlord looks at him quizzically when he comes down the stairs.

'A good night, young sir?'

'Thank you. Yes. In all the circumstances.'

'You were none too clear last night about who you were, but I recognised my brother's writing on the paper you gave me. I've a hunch that, as to actually just how you got here, you haven't got a clue.'

'Well, no. I haven't, as a matter of fact. My head aches like hell and I feel very peculiar.'

'You were brought here by a young gentleman who said you're a drover and he'd travelled down with you from Wales. He said he'd bumped into you in Covent Garden and at least you'd had the presence of mind to show him my brother's note. He brought you here and paid me to take you in. I wasn't keen at first, I can tell you.'

'Robert? Robert Williams?'

'Aye, that's him. Told me to tell you he didn't go on his Grand Tour after all, as his uncle told him it was too dangerous, what with revolutionary France and wars everywhere else. He would have stayed, but he had to get back to his own lodgings as he was booked on the early coach back up to Wales. Wishes you good luck. Really nice man, he was.'

'Look, thanks for taking me in. I do appreciate it and tonight I'll be in a much better state, I promise you!'

'Well, I'll drink to that, but *you* really shouldn't!'

After a rather pleasant stroll through the streets towards Covent Garden and feeling more confident about knowing where he is and where he's going, Rhys arrives at the theatre. His head aches less than it did and he hopes that no more headaches await him after his shameful evening the night before.

Arriving at the front door and announcing himself, he is promptly told to go round to the back of the building down an alley, where he'll find the stage door. From there, the stage door manager gets a young boy to accompany him to Mr Sheridan's office. He nimbly leads Rhys along various narrow corridors and up several flights of stairs.

'It's a swanky office, sir. Some say it cost a small fortune to fit out. 'Undreds of pounds.'

'That's rather a lot for one room, isn't it?'

'That's nuffin! The whole place has cost Mr Sheridan over fifty thousand pounds. We don't let just anyone in here, you know. Last week…'

At this point they arrive at the office and, finding the door open, enter a very well-appointed room, richly furnished with a large wooden desk, a lavish drinks table and sumptuous red brocade curtains at the windows. They see Richard Sheridan, dressed in what must be his trademark green, thinks Rhys, in residence behind his desk with a large schooner of drink in front of him.

'Ah, Rhys. You're early. Sir Charlton is yet to come. No matter. A glass of Madeira?'

The boy sniggers.

'You can scarper. And don't let anyone up here.'

' 'Ceptin' Sir Charlton, I'm supposin', sir!'

'Of course Sir Charlton, you cheeky young fool. Now, be off with you before I box your ears. And shut that door!'

The boy leaves, slamming the door behind him.

'The varmint!'

'He seems like a bright young lad to me.'

'Too big for his boots, but yes, he's a quick learner though he does get a bit above himself. I could hear you coming up the stairs – this whole place echoes – and yes, he's right about the new theatre putting me in debt all right.'

'And costing fifty thousand pounds.'

'Actually it cost more than double the original estimate so fifty thousand is on the low side in fact.'

'I'm sorry. I can't comprehend so much money.'

'Well yes, it's a lot, and that's why I'm glad you signed this contract with me. I'm relying on your show with Sir Charlton to help me a bit financially.'

'Wait a minute. I know I was probably the worse for wear last night, but I signed a contract with Sir Charlton. At least I thought that was what I was doing.'

'No, no no! It's a contract with me, with the theatre. Charlton knows that. But it amounts to the same thing. You and he run the show.'

With that, there is a loud knock on the door and it is flung open by the boy who grandly announces that there is a visitor. In walks a very cheerful and full-of-himself Sir Charlton.

'Morning, Richard! Good morning, Rhys. Slept well I trust?'

'I was lucky to get back to my lodgings for the night, Sir Charlton. You really should have stopped me drinking so much.'

'It's for a man to know his own limits!'

'Well, one limit is this contract. I want to see it again before I agree to it.'

'Too late for that,' interjects Richard.

'Way too late. You signed it before witnesses. There was no coercion,' adds Sir Charlton, 'and anyway, you want to do the show, don't you?'

'Yes, I think so, but not under any terms.'

'The terms are good. Very good. Share of the box office, which Sir Charlton's men run. At least he knows what's what, don't you, Charlton. He's looked after your joint interests just fine.'

'Shake hands with your new partner.'

With those words, Sir Charlton extends a bulbous hand to Rhys who reluctantly reaches out his own to seal the deal with a gentleman's handshake.

Richard pours them both a drink and gestures for them to sit down.

'Let's celebrate and get down to talking about the show. You were planning it last night and not just signing contracts, I hope?'

Talking about the show excites Rhys and he quickly sets aside worries about the agreement. He puts it and the image of a disapproving Honesty clean out of his head, especially when his two backers take him in to have a look at the inside of the theatre.

It takes his breath away. Ornate and magnificent, with five tiers, the auditorium is vast. Standing on the huge stage, Rhys is transfixed by the scale of it and humbled by the realisation that he is to perform in such a place.

37

Some days later

REHEARSALS ARE GOING WELL. With only a couple of days left before the first of five nights, Rhys is sitting taking a breath of not-so-fresh London air outside the theatre when he is clapped on the back. He tries to turn round, only to be smothered in a bear hug by Honesty.

'Am I pleased to see you, Rhys. I've had the devil of a job to find you. I was sent to The Magpie and then on to here.'

'I knew you'd find me. How was Kent?'

'My brother was the same as ever, constantly scoring points and doing everything to convince me that his life is better than mine, but it was good to see him. I know he misses Wales, so I forgive him trying to sound cheerful about his new life. Still, never mind me, what is going on with you?'

Rhys tells Honesty what has happened, glossing over the contract story that niggles him into an embarrassingly brief retelling of events since Honesty and he had last seen each other.

'That sounds incredible, Rhys. You're going to be the star of the show, I'm sure. You'll not come home after this, will you?'

'I plan to. I'll have to. Anyway, I'll need to collect the balance of monies from Laycock, won't I?'

'Yes, in a week's time, he says. I called in to see him on my way to your Smithfield lair. Prices are going up all the time, but he needs to shift the remnants of our herd. I told him where you are, so you can wait until he comes to find you.'

'You'll stay for the show, won't you?'

'I can't, Rhys, I'm sorry. I have to get back. I've all manner of business to complete here in London before going home to sort things out at that end. We'll need the extra monies back as soon as Laycock can hand it over to you in a week or so, so you had better be ready to make a hasty departure or things could get awkward for me.'

Sir Charlton comes out of the theatre entrance, sees Rhys and shouts over.

'Come on, Rhys, you're due on stage for a run through of the whole show. Is that old boy bothering you?'

'Righto, Sir Charlton.'

Rhys turns to Honesty, 'Sorry about that, he's all bluster, but I'd better be off.'

'So had I, Rhys, so had I. I'll not get involved with the likes of him. You can have that dubious honour. Farewell, Rhys, and do Wales proud.'

'I'll try my very best, Honesty, and try not to let you down with Laycock either.'

One final shake of hands and they both turn to go their very separate ways.

38

THE DAY OF THE FIRST performance arrives. The tickets have all sold out in advance. Rhys realises that, more than anything else, this is probably on the strength of the Prince of Wales being announced as attending every performance. Thanks for that have been duly accorded to Edward Jones by Richard Sheridan, who looks less careworn every day. The show is billed as:

A Grand Selection of Welsh and Patriotic Music and Verse
Over Five Consecutive Nights with the
Nightly Attendance of the Prince of Wales

— with the names of all the performers set out in full in the three parts of the evening's entertainment.

In the end, of course, Edward Jones has been prevailed upon to perform and he takes over some of the programme from Rhys. Peeved though he is by this, Rhys can hardly complain as Edward has provided the royal patronage and has personally cajoled all the performers, including Rhys, to take part.

From performance to performance, Rhys grows in confidence. One review has it that: 'Rhys Morgan is the real star and is the musical and performing personification of *hiraeth* – that curious Welsh word with no English translation that means a longing for one's homeland, but is really a yearning for the unattainable.'

Another reviewer remarks that: 'You may be able to take the singer, Rhys Morgan, out of Wales, but you cannot take Wales out of the singer.'

Rhys manages his after-show appearances each night at Bedford's with greater confidence and less embarrassment than at his debut there.

Raucous and riotous encores of some of the most popular songs at the theatre are demanded by the revellers at the coffeehouse, including *All Through the Night*, *Forth to the Battle*, *The Men of Harlech* and *The Bells of Aberdovey*.

Rhys is persuaded by shouts and foot-stomping to round off each night's drinking with one last rendition of the achingly beautiful tune, *David of the White Rock*, with which he nightly steals the show at the theatre.

Over a plaintive harp introduction, he first tells the story of the harpist David Owen who calls for his harp as he lies dying in bed and whose final act is to play a haunting melody he composes on the spot and, when finished, to die.

Rhys then sings words he has put to the tune, telling the story in a beautifully poetic way of the dying composer's last wish. Each night he puts in more and more verses when performing the piece, driving the listeners to higher and higher levels of sadness.

In actual fact, Rhys himself is being driven to greater and greater levels of sadness by the lyrics at the realisation that whilst he has found contentment playing and singing on the stage, he is also losing his will to return home.

As he sings about David of the White Rock calling for his harp one last time, it is as if Rhys is seeing himself lying on his own death bed with Eunice and his father at his side.

Because of this, it's always with a heavy heart that Rhys returns late to The Magpie from the nightly celebrations of the success of the show.

Nevertheless, Sir Charlton persuades him to perform for an extra night, with tickets to be sold on the door.

Edward withdraws from this additional show, pleading overwhelming exhaustion, but suggests that some of his solo performances be taken over by Rhys, who, he helpfully says, can do all the accompaniment for the other artistes.

He also suggests that they ask his friend, Iolo Morganwyg, to perform some poetry from his book *Poems Lyric and Pastoral*.

Crowds and crowds in disorderly queues throng the foyer and the streets outside for this extra night's performance. Fights and scuffles break out, but Sir Charlton's men – many more of them than usual – manage to keep order.

A great deal of money is taken on the door and the curtain is delayed because of the chaos that ensues in the clamour for tickets.

Rhys is oblivious to all of this backstage and finds himself drawn in by the charisma of Iolo, who holds sway in the Green Room.

The show goes exceptionally well until towards the end when Iolo, after reciting some of the poems of the ancient poet, Dafydd ap Gwilym, which are well received, decides to live up to his name as the Bard of Liberty. He breaks into a lecture on the evils of the slave trade – going so far as to say that people should avoid eating sweet things tainted with the gore of the slavery that produces the sugar – and, to boos, starts reciting a poem that he first dedicates to his friend, Humanity's Wilberforce. He then loudly proclaims:

Join here thy Bards, with mournful note,
They weep for AFRIC's injur'd race;
Long has thy MUSE in worlds remote
Sang loud of BRITAIN'S foul disgrace.

In the wings, Richard Sheridan is anxious to remove Iolo from the stage and forces Rhys to go on and start playing his harp. Rhys does so, but only to give Iolo encouragement and musical accompaniment.

They both refuse to leave and the audience gradually responds positively to both men as they perform together and win the crowd round.

The show ends with the audience shouting for more and the theatre has to close its iron safety curtain to signal the end of the evening's entertainment – as well as prevent the boisterous audience from storming the stage.

That evening at Bedford's is a wild one, with several Welsh poets, en route to Paris to see the revolution in progress, staying to catch up with Iolo. Rhys is totally absorbed in the mood and gets caught up in their fervour. Even Iolo's friend William Wilberforce drops by and 'Liberty for all' is toasted time after time. Rhys thinks nothing of the fact that Sir Charlton does not appear, as he knows he is a dyed-in-the-wool Tory and aristocrat, unable to cut the ties that bind him and unwilling to be seen to hobnob with radicals.

39

It is only when Rhys is roused by his landlord the day after the night before, that he suddenly realises he might have a problem.

'Wake up, Rhys. This is serious. A Mr Richard Sheridan, or so he says, is downstairs. He wants to know where Sir Charlton is. You'd better get dressed and come downstairs quick. He's got five very ugly-looking customers with him, keen to come and wake you themselves.'

'What's happened? Did he say?'

Rhys is up and getting dressed as he listens to the answer.

'Your man Sir Charlton has done a bunk.'

'What d'you mean? Absconded?'

'Skedaddled with all the takings from last night. Mr Sheridan clearly thinks you're in on it. I assured him you were here and are too honest for that.'

With that, the door is flung open and in burst two large men, followed closely by Richard Sheridan.

'Rhys. Where the hell is Sir Charlton and where the hell is my money?'

'Where the hell, indeed? Don't forget that it's my money too. My week's share was coming out of that.'

'Never mind that. I need that money badly. I can't find him and nobody seems to know where he is. When did you last see him?'

'Last night, of course.'

'After the performance?'

'Well, no actually. He came backstage during the performance.'

'What did he say?'

'He was angry that Iolo was performing. Said it would ruin his reputation. Come to think of it, he wasn't at Bedford's either, but because of what he'd said about Iolo I didn't think anything was amiss.'

'That bloody Bard of Liberty.'

'It's hardly his fault. He's not taken the money.'

'No, I thought it was you with Sir Charlton. All the way here, I kept thinking of the name of the inn you were lodging in and thinking it was a perfect hideaway for a thieving magpie.'

'I resent that, Mr Sheridan. I give you my word, it has nothing to do with me. I'm as outraged as you are and just as cheated. What can be done?'

'Well, for a start, you've given me more than your word. You've given me your signature on this contract and these bailiff's men will help me extract what I can from you.

'We'll have your harp, for a start. And the horse you've told me you've left outside London. Then we'll have a word with that man Laycock that you've been telling me – and everyone else stupid enough to listen to you – about, and how he's selling the rest of your herd. When he sees this contract, he'll have to pay us and not you.'

'I only signed to appear on the stage.'

'You did more than that. You signed as guarantor for the booking of the theatre. I'll make you pay.'

'You can't do that!'

'Oh, can't I? We'll soon see about that. It's either pay up or it's the Fleet debtors' prison for you. Take him, lads.'

Rhys has his arms pinned behind him and his harp is taken, but he manages to shout to the innkeeper.

'Tell your brother what's happened. Tell him to send word somehow to Honesty.'

'What about my money for a week's food and lodging?'

'I'll see you get paid. Honest. That's a promise.'

Rhys is manhandled downstairs, out into the street, and bundled violently into the waiting horse-drawn carriage. He senses that his whole world is crumbling.

'This can't be happening. Not to me. Mr Sheridan, I give you my word that I know nothing of all this and I'll do anything to help you get to the bottom of it. Sir Charlton is a complete rogue to have done this to you. And to me. Just tell me what I can do and I'll do it.'

Richard Sheridan is calmer now.

'Rhys. The contract is the contract. Any court of law will uphold it, no matter what you say about not knowing what you were signing. I accept that you're not party to this dastardly embezzlement, especially as you have so much to lose, but I'll be severely out of pocket over this and I've debts of my own to pay.'

'I'll perform for nothing to pay it off. You can't take the money from Laycock. It will ruin so many people, never mind me.'

'I'm sorry. This is the way of the world. I've got to protect myself. I can't think about everyone else. That's what contracts are for.'

'But it's fraud. It can't be right. Have mercy, I beg you.'

'I can't. I can't afford to be merciful. And I can't be seen to be running the theatre like a school for scandal!'

Pleased with his own joke, Richard Sheridan, smugly but gently, laughs at his handling of this undoubted problem and Rhys falls silent, digesting the dimension of his own disgrace.

It is a slow and painful journey up to Islington and seems to pass in a dream, as does the encounter with Laycock. At first he is pleased to see Rhys, but after explanations are given, he ends up disgusted at having to hand the balance of the money from the sale of the herd to a theatrical.

'You know this will ruin Honesty, don't you. And you're finished, Rhys. You'll be lucky even to be taken in back at home.'

'I know that, Mr Laycock. Only too well.'

'Honesty told me you were work in progress and I see now what he means. Did he not tell you to trust no one and be surprised when they don't let you down, rather than trust everyone and be doomed to a life of disappointment when they do?'

'Well, I assumed as Sir Charlton had been born to it, he would have a certain moral code to live by.'

'Rhys, Rhys, Rhys. The more the outside embellishment, the less the inner man. I suppose you've learnt that from all this, if nothing else. I take it you'll be going home to face the music?'

'He'll be working off his debts to me for some considerable time to come, Mr Laycock,' Richard emphasises, signalling to his men to take hold of Rhys and get him back into the coach.

'Don't worry, Mr Laycock, I've arranged for a message to get to Honesty.'

The coach takes the group back to the theatre and Rhys is escorted to the upstairs office where Richard is soon seated at his desk with his captive audience opposite.

'Rhys, I like you. I want you to perform here from time to time. I'll pay your board and lodging and a few pence more. That way, I reckon, in a few months we'll call it quits. After that, we can review arrangements and maybe pay you more.'

'That's reasonable of you in all the circumstances, I suppose, but I now have a massive debt to Honesty. This'll come as a bitter blow to him, to say nothing of what it will do to my father and the other farmers who will be hard hit.

'The irony of it all is that, love the theatre as I do, I'd come round to the view that it's all froth. I am only any good because I've got Wales inside me and, to keep that, I now know more than ever before that I need to be inside Wales.

'Look at Edward Jones. He's been an exile for far too long. That's why he looks permanently lost. Honesty saw that in him right away.

'And my girl Eunice. I've not treated her properly at all. Too late, I've realised that she's a diamond in the rough and I have failed to see her true qualities.'

'Rhys, I had no idea you could be so eloquent. Maybe you should be writing plays for me too. You'd pay off your debt even quicker if you did.'

'I'm no playwright, Mr Sheridan. Poet maybe. But it's a poor bard that can be as insensitive as I've been – only thinking about myself and making my way in the world, without thinking about the things that made me and my world.'

'There you go again, Rhys, a turn of phrase worthy of a wordsmith.'

40

Some time later

A LETTER REACHES HONESTY. He is stunned by its contents and rushes to Caradog's farm, banging on the farmhouse door until it is opened by the flustered and pale occupant.

'What brings you here in such a rush, Honesty?'

'Caradog, you'd better sit down.'

'What's happened to Rhys?'

'All in good time, all in good time.'

The two men sit either side of the fire.

'Caradog. Rhys is alive. No worry on that score. Thankfully, I suppose.'

'What do you mean by that exactly?'

'Well, I'm not sure what to make of it. It appears that Rhys signed as surety to a debt and has been forced to pay the price. The balance of the herd money from Laycock has been distrained and Rhys still owes more. He cannot return until it's paid up in full or it's debtors' prison for him.'

Carodog slumps in his seat and, visibly shocked and moved, he sighs, holding his chest.

'I thought you said he was doing well and was set fair to appear on the stage and then return. This is worse than any of my worst fears. We can't tell Eunice.'

'Too late! I'm already here,' comes a voice comes from the hall.

Honesty stands to acknowledge her entry to the room as she kneels at Carodog's feet and takes his hand.

'Eunice, you were not meant to find this out now. Not like this.'

'I knew something might happen. I thought London would change Rhys. I thought it might ensnare him. I didn't think he would lose his way quite so badly. You can see how frail Carodog is now. These past few weeks he has steadily gone downhill and this latest turn of events will not help. With Rhys not returning, I'm staying here most nights now to keep an eye on him.'

Carodog rallies as he tries to regain his composure.

'Honesty. What's to be done? I'll sell the farm. Or I'll sign it over to you. You must be paid. And all the others.

My good name. Your good name, for heaven's sake. They're worth more. And what good is the farm to me now. I'm too ill to work it and Rhys is a reluctant farmer at the best of times. Now he's lost. All is lost to me now.'

'Caradog, I shouldn't have come straight to tell you the bad news without having thought about a solution. That just makes me part of the problem. Do nothing hasty. Let me think about it.'

'I'll write to Rhys, if you give me the address where he is staying,' says Eunice. She stands up at the same time as Honesty and they both walk to the front door where they converse in whispered tones.

'I had no idea Caradog was weakening so fast. He is much worse than when I last saw him. You are doing a fine job caring for him. I'm only sorry I didn't bring Rhys back when I had the chance, but he was determined to stay and, of course, it was a chance to get more money for the herd with him on hand to wait to collect. It's my greed, Eunice. I'm to blame, to be honest.'

'Nonsense, Honesty. Rhys was greedy for happiness through his music and hungry for fame and fortune. It seems you can't have them all at the same time.'

'Let me see what I can do. We can't let Caradog sell the farm.'

'No, I'm feared that might kill him.'

41

HONESTY'S NEXT CALL IS ON Sir Hugh Williams and he is pleasantly surprised to find Robert back and standing in the hall by the front door as he is admitted by a member of the household staff.

'Robert! How lovely to see you. I'd heard that you'd abandoned your Grand Tour. How does it feel to be back?'

'Quite frankly, Honesty, I'm glad. The drove was education enough. I think I might come on the next one!'

'Well you'd be an asset, that's for sure.'

'What brings you here? Business with my father, no doubt?'

'Yes. Serious business. Stay and listen.'

'That sounds intriguing. I'll get my father directly.'

Robert goes off up the wide wooden staircase and soon reappears with his father who, after a few pleasantries, takes them both into his vast study with views down to the Menai Strait to the exact spot where the drove had started all those weeks ago.

Honesty explains what has happened, interrupted by the offer and the pouring of large sherries and then the gasps of astonishment at the news.

It's clear that Honesty and Sir Hugh have a great trust and understanding. At the end of the story, the drover stands.

'So you see, I can't let Caradog sell his farm. I'll sell mine first to pay off the other farmers and the balance I owe you for your head of cattle.'

'Honesty. It is typical of you, not just to say that, but to mean every word. There'll be no need for that. You saved me a small fortune by outsmarting that rogue Windle. Forget about what you owe me and I'll pay the other farmers and settle with you and Caradog into the bargain.

'It's Rhys, from what you say, that is our concern now and the worry about him that risks his father's health. I know how that feels having worried about Robert when he was away and knowing the relief of having him back here at home and safe.

'You and Caradog have been the mainstay of farming and droving in this area throughout my life and you've both helped me in more ways than I can ever repay. This is the least I can do.'

'Sir, I'm truly honoured that you feel this way and I'm eternally grateful for your kindness. If I'm able to clear my name sufficiently, it'll mean that the bank idea can go ahead with me part of it. I'll see to it that shares are given to you, which should see a return of your capital in thanks for your generous restitution of my honour.'

'Very well, Honesty, and a fair proposal. Give the shares to Robert here. And maybe you can find him a job with the bank – although he seems smitten with droving and all it entails. But your priority now is to get Rhys home. I'm told he has considerable talents as a poet and musician. He belongs here, not in London.'

'Aye, sir. Right enough.'

42

HONESTY PLANS HIS NEXT MOVE CAREFULLY. He consults
with nobody, but walks and thinks all day, and tosses, turns
and thinks all night, revisiting how to proceed.

After a few days of this, he calls on Guto to find him
preparing for a journey.

'Where are you off to, Guto?'

'To see Mair. It's time I did some proper courting.'

'Well, for once I agree with you.'

'But what else is on your mind, Honesty. I've heard
about Rhys and what a bloody stupid fool he's been. It's
all anybody round here is talking about. Well, that and
how it's slowly causing Caradog to fade away.'

'I'm not sure how Eunice is really coping either, mind
you. Running around after the old man is keeping her

from thinking about what all this means for her. Anyway, I can see you want to be off and you've a long journey ahead of you. I'm here because I want you to do me a favour. You don't *have* to do it, but I would be extremely grateful if you could.'

'Come on, Honesty, spit it out, I haven't got all day.'

'Fetch Rhys back for me.'

'What?'

'Bring him home. He'll be down and disheartened. Ashamed too, I'd warrant. I've wrestled with the idea of going down myself, but I suspect that wouldn't work. I know from further letters that he and others have sent me that he's in a bad way and ashamed at having let us all down, especially me. You two formed some kind of bond – much to my surprise, I admit. Maybe you can talk some sense into him. Knock it into him if needs be.

'Look, I have a letter here for Richard Laycock. He'll help you, I know. I have some cash here and letters of credit too. I've put some money together which might help to get Rhys out of debt. Apparently he was talking about debtors' prison and all kinds.'

'I'm not sure, Honesty. I've got my work cut out convincing Mair to marry me, never mind persuading Rhys to come home. I'm not sure what to say to him or what to do to deal with his creditors.'

'Don't worry, I've written instructions here for you too.'

'You thought I'd do your dirty work for you then? A bit ahead of yourself, aren't you?'

'Guto, I know that beneath that hard exterior of yours is a soft understanding. You won't let us down, I'm sure of that.'

'Oh, all right then. It seems I've no choice. I'll do it. Come by this afternoon and you can tell me all I need to know. I'll be leaving first thing in the morning.'

Honesty leaves Guto to his final preparations and goes to tell Caradog and Eunice the good news.

However, that's not how they treat it.

Carodog is adamant about selling the farm and not taking a penny from Honesty.

He's not sure Rhys will return and he's not at all sure about facing him, even if he does.

Eunice tearfully explains that, as Rhys has not written to her, or made any efforts to contact her, she must assume he no longer feels the same way about her.

Honesty leaves them in poor spirits, with Eunice confiding to him at the door that Caradog's will is broken and she herself is in despair.

Nothing Honesty can say seems to help either of them.

43

A couple of weeks later

IT IS SOME TIME, even after reaching London, before Guto catches up with Rhys. He finds him at The Magpie, working as a pot washer and looking very thin and gaunt.

Not recognising him at first, Guto asks the innkeeper for the whereabouts of Rhys Morgan, only to be pointed in the direction of a shabby fellow cleaning the tables. Rhys has heard his name and turns to face his searcher.

'Hello, stranger. Come to laugh at my downfall?'

'That's not how I see it, Rhys.'

'How do you see it, Guto? The facts are simple: a fool from Wales and his money – actually other people's money – are soon parted. Drover welshes on his debts.

Musician brings disgrace to his friends and family…need I go on.'

'Well, all of that, I suppose, is true, but we know you, Rhys. That's not you. It's what's happened to you, yes. You've been a fool, yes, but you were duped by all accounts. Could've happened to anybody.'

'Not anybody, Guto. Me. It had to happen to a fool who played the harp and thought he could sing and write poetry.'

'That's also true, of course. But you can still do those things. You haven't lost that along with everything else.'

'Young man,' joined the innkeeper, 'I'm afraid you're wrong there. Rhys was thrown out of the Theatre Royal a week or so back, booed off the stage.

'Mr Sheridan brought him here a complete wreck and told me he'd not likely ever perform there again barring a miracle. A series of sell-out performances and then one catastrophic night and they throw you out.'

'What happened?' Guto looks from the innkeeper back to Rhys.

'I've finished with music and it's finished with me. I went to pieces playing all that Welsh music. It tugged at my heartstrings too much. Night after night, putting my heart and soul into it, it got too much for me, I suppose.

'All I kept thinking was that I'd turned my back on all I'd ever loved and sold out to the devil. Only my sacred harp was true and playing it plucked out my soul until

I became an empty shell. The emotion of the songs and everything they stand for proved too much for me in the end.

'I went to pieces, forgot all my words and just stood there alone on the stage with the booing and jeering echoing loudly in my ears.'

The innkeeper glances at him anxiously and Guto notices that he's obviously looking out for Rhys as he joins in the conversation.

'At least he got his harp back from Drury Lane. Sometimes I can get him to play it here and it goes down well with my regular customers. I want him to get his nerve back, so he can show those theatre so-called gentlemen that he can perform again and pay off the rest of his debt.

'Until then he's doing odd jobs for me to earn his keep. He shuffles about here most of the time, but the music can still work a bit of magic on him and the customers.'

Guto is shocked and takes Rhys by the arm.

'I think Rhys and I should pay Mr Sheridan a visit, don't you, Mr Landlord?'

'Indeed I do. It needs somebody to turn things around or else…'

'Enough said. Rhys, let's go right now. How long will it take to get there, landlord?'

'Not long. Rhys knows the way, after all.'

On the way, Rhys explains how it all happened and what has gone on in the time since they last met.

44

WHEN THEY ARRIVE AT THE THEATRE, the errand boy is pleased to see Rhys, but puzzled to see him in his present forlorn state. As he takes them from the stage door up the narrow staircases, he chatters away with the visitors.

'You was one of my favourites. Can't think what's happened to you. That night you got the catcalls you just...'

'Dried... that's what theatricals call it. A polite way of saying that I completely lost what I was doing.'

'Well Mr Sheridan misses you, that's for sure. They've tried other Welsh nights, but without you or Mr Jones they don't work.'

'Who is Mr Jones,' Guto asks.

'That's Edward Jones, royal harpist. He got me into all this.'

'Then surely he can get you out of it?'

'No. That's the trouble. With the Prince of Wales on his side you'd think so, but he has debts himself and can't help.'

'Refuses to help, you mean.'

'Well, either way…'

They arrive at the office, the boy knocks on the door and they enter when they hear 'Come!' being shouted from within.

Richard Sheridan is putting down his half-empty glass as he stands to greet them.

'Rhys. This is an unexpected pleasure.'

'Is it?' replies Rhys, clearly disenchanted with such pleasantries.

'Most certainly. Are you come to tell me you are ready to get back on the horse and start performing for me again?'

Guto steps forward and leans on the desk.

'Actually, he'll be getting back on his horse all right, but it'll be to come home to Wales with me, Mr Sheridan.'

'How so? I still have the contract and his debt to me is still, shall we say, significant.'

'I would like to see that contract if you please, as apart from you and Rhys and that scallywag Sir Charlton…'

Guto is now leaning more threateningly over the desk.

'Why certainly, Mr, Mr…?'

'I'm Guto, but you can call me Mr Jenkins.'

'I have it right here.'

He flicks through some papers on his desk and, locating the contract in question, passes it to Guto.

Guto takes up the contract and studies it.

'This the only copy?'

'Yes it is. So I'll thank you to hand it back if you've finished.'

'The only copy…'

With a couple of movements, Guto is tearing at the contract and walking towards the fireplace in the corner of the room. In next to no time, the contract is burning on the fire as Richard Sheridan leaps to his feet and tries to get past Guto who elbows him aside.

'What the hell… stop! Boy. Do something. Don't just stand there.'

Guto spins round with his gun in his hand.

'Stand there is what you'll do. Over there.'

Rhys is horrified at this turn of events.

'Guto, you can't do this. It's breaking the law.'

'Well, I've just done it. This contract is now void. I have twenty guineas for you, Mr Sheridan. That should settle things. Honesty says that you've more or less had Rhys indentured as a slave, totally illegally in his view.'

'I can take this to court, you know,' says Sheridan, 'and seek justice and a proper financial recompense.'

'Or you can take this more than fair payment in full and final settlement. Or I can use this gun. Your choice.'

'There's no need for that. I'll take the money. But, Rhys, it means your theatre days are over. I'll see to it that you never work the stage again. How will you live without it?'

'It may come as a surprise to you, Mr Sheridan, but the real drama in life happens off the stage.'

'Yes, but some, like you, were born to be on it.'

'He'll survive,' says Guto. 'And now, so will you. Don't try any more legal business. It's only your word against ours as to what the terms of that document were and a court case will do you no favours, I can assure you.

'And what you've been paid in kind by Rhys, and now in cash by me, is more than enough to relieve Rhys of his debt to you. But one last thing. Where is Sir Charlton Musgrove?'

'I… I… I don't rightly know. I'm not in touch with him any more.'

Guto turns to Rhys.

'Come on, Rhys. Let's go. This place is getting me down. It's more like Dreary Lane to me.'

They leave, with the boy trailing behind them, whispering.

'He still sees Sir Charlton. Every night at Bedford's and sometimes in the mornings here. They've made it up as, in the end, Sir Charlton paid Mr Sheridan a share of the extra night's performance — said he'd had gambling debts to pay and urgently needed all the takings at the time. I've heard them chuckling at how they had tricked Rhys with the contract, but you didn't hear that from me.'

Guto bristles at this and realises they've all been tricked. He turns to go back past Rhys, up the stairs, his wild eyes flashing in fury.

Rhys restrains him. 'Leave it, Guto, let's go before we make matters worse.'

Reluctantly, Guto turns again and they descend the stairs in silence.

Outside the theatre, Rhys turns to Guto.

'I should be grateful, Guto.'

'I should hope so too.'

'And I am, of course. But I feel even more ashamed that you've had to bail me out.'

'It's what friends are for, Rhys. And what this friend would like to do right now is, well, let's go and visit this rogue, Sir Charlton what's 'is name.'

'Let's not, Guto. It could turn ugly. He's involved with a nasty crowd. It's over now, let's just call it a day and get back to The Magpie.'

'Righto. I guess we could both do with a drink.'

As they make their way from Covent Garden to Smithfield, they discuss what has just happened and Rhys wonders if they will get away with it.

'Rhys, I'm certain. It's a good deal for him and he knows it. And we know he didn't really lose out at all now he's made up with his partner in crime. I'm not even sure how he or Sir Charlton can spread rumours about you without implicating themselves. Nobody would come out of it well.'

'I suppose you're right. So thanks, Guto. I'm in your debt. Where did you get the twenty guineas? I'll see you get it back. Honest.'

'Ah, glad you said that. It was Honesty who put me up to this. It's him you owe, not me. I'd have left you to rot down here.'

'Honesty eh? But how can I ever repay him?'

'Don't worry, I'm sure he'll have thought about that too. Let's just get you back so you can thank him yourself.'

'I can't come back, Guto. I can't face my father. Or Eunice. Or anybody for that matter.'

'I'm sorry to say this, Rhys, but you're father is very ill. Eunice is nursing him. She's not sure how long he's got. Honesty says they are both much changed by what has happened.

'You have to return to see them even if you can't put matters right. I'm to pay off your debts down here with the innkeeper and anybody else and then get you home. That's my job. Don't make me use force, Rhys, but I will if I have to.

'And, anyway, I want you back home as well, for what it's worth. We've got our own business to attend to.'

45

Some time later

Rhys and Guto arrive home in Wales after an eventful journey. After stops with Mair and her family and at some of the various inns they had stayed at on their drove down to London, they finally arrive at Honesty's homestead. Rhys is puzzled as to why Guto is insistent they go there first rather than straight to his father's farm.

It is a very sheepish Rhys that greets Honesty when he opens his door.

'Well, well, well. The wanderers are back. Good job, Guto. Thanks for obeying orders and bringing him to me. I assume I am the first port of call. Come in, boys. Come in.'

In the kitchen by the fire, Guto briefly recounts his London experiences and Honesty turns to Rhys.

'You're quiet, Rhys.'

'Is it any wonder? I didn't want to return. Well I did want to come back, but felt I had let too many people down — especially you, Honesty — and I couldn't think how I would face my father. Or Eunice. I've failed them both. I couldn't even bring myself to write to them, even though I had the most touching letter from Eunice. That makes me feel so ashamed.'

'You'll have some fences to mend all round, that's for sure. But forgiving and forgetting is the way forward. However, I have to prepare you for the worst, Rhys. Your father has only a few days left, we think. Eunice has seen a rapid decline.'

'Does he want to see me?'

'Rhys, don't be ridiculous. He longs to see you. He wanted to sell the farm to get you back. He blames himself for forcing you into droving. None of us can tell him any different. When I explained what me and Guto were up to, he even insisted on signing the farm over to me, but never fear, I told him I would sign it over to you when I thought you were ready.'

'I must go to him straight away.'

'Yes, you must. But Eunice. She's very upset indeed by what's happened. She'll take some convincing that you and she can take up where you left off. And, Rhys, what'll you say to persuade her?'

'I read some wise words in *The Observer* when I was at my lowest in London and they struck a chord with me. A Scottish doctor and poet called Alexander Chalmers wrote, 'The three grand essentials of happiness are: something to do, someone to love, and something to hope for.'

Both Honesty and Guto look at each other and nod in approval as Rhys continues.

'You see, I've learnt much in these past months and thanks to your offer for Guto and me to take over, then the droving experience itself and the letters you sent, they all gave me comfort even before I was rescued by Guto, thanks again to you.

'Knowing the friendship and loyalty I have back home, I know this is where I want to be. I will be a farmer and a drover from now on. There will always be music in my life, but I've realised that for life to be my music, I must live the life I know I love. And that's here, with Eunice.

'Yes, I still have hopes for my music, but here in Wales. My only real ambition now is to be true to myself and others. If I can do that, I now realise, it will be my greatest achievement.'

'Well, that's settled,' Honesty says. 'You must go home, but first, Guto, tell us what happened between you and Mair.'

'We are to be wed. I am to work with her father, but don't panic! I will still be free to do the droving with Rhys and will come back to Wales at the start of each drove and hold his hand all the way to London… and back!'

Honesty could not be more pleased as they all set off for Caradog's farm.

46

A FEW DAYS AFTER RHYS'S RETURN, Caradog dies. They had been reconciled within moments of the prodigal son's return.

Eunice and Rhys had, on first sight, realised they could not let recriminations cloud their feelings for each other and embraced at once.

The old man's dying wish is that Rhys plays the harp and sings at his funeral.

Rhys alone knows what he is going to play and in the small chapel, full to the rafters, he steps forward to perform *The Hall of my Chieftain* in an emotional musical tribute to the man who had been, until then, the unsung hero of his household.

The hall of my chieftain is gloomy tonight,
I weep for the grave has extinguish'd its light:
The beam of its lamp from the summit is o'er
The blaze of its hearth shall give welcome no more.

The hall of my chieftain is voiceless and still,
The sound of its harpings hath died on the hill!
Be silent for ever, thou desolate scene,
Nor let e'en an echo recall what hath been!

The hall of my chieftain is lonely and bare
No banquet, no guest, not a footstep is there!
Oh! Where are the warriors who circled its board?
The grass will soon wave where the mead-cup was pour'd.

The hall of my chieftain is loveless to-night,
Since he is departed whose smile made it bright:
I mourn, but the sigh of my soul shall be brief,
The pathway is short to the grave of my chief!'

Carodog is then buried in a small cemetery overlooking the Menai Strait. The drovers gather round Rhys and Eunice and, at one point, they all turn to look to the other shore. The men think of their next drove but Rhys sees his father on the far side, standing there, waving, in the distance.

This time, leaving *him* behind.